"He was conceived on our wedding night."

He had a son? Just like that? One moment alone in the world, the next moment, a son?

Very slowly, he lowered his hand until the backs of his fingers grazed the baby's round cheek. How could skin be that soft?

His son. *Nathan.*

"Will you lift him for me?" she said, glancing at him.

He nodded. And just like that, he lifted his son for the first time, careful to put one hand behind the little guy's heavy head. The baby kicked and squirmed and Brady held on tight, terrified he'd drop him.

"Relax," Lara said. "You're doing fine. Just comfort him. Hold him closer. Don't be afraid."

He pulled Nathan against his chest, one hand all but covering the small boy's back. Then he tipped him away from his chest for a moment, anxious to really look at this few pounds of humanity that instantly redefined his life.

ALICE SHARPE

THE LAWMAN'S SECRET SON

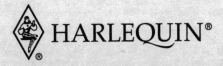

HARLEQUIN®

TORONTO • NEW YORK • LONDON
AMSTERDAM • PARIS • SYDNEY • HAMBURG
STOCKHOLM • ATHENS • TOKYO • MILAN • MADRID
PRAGUE • WARSAW • BUDAPEST • AUCKLAND

This book couldn't have been written without
the patient support of my son, Officer Joseph Sharpe
(mistakes are mine, not his), and is dedicated, with love,
to his wonderful daughter, Carmen Amelia Sharpe.

ISBN-13: 978-0-373-69343-6
ISBN-10:   0-373-69343-5

THE LAWMAN'S SECRET SON

Printed in U.S.A.

ABOUT THE AUTHOR

Alice Sharpe met her husband-to-be on a cold, foggy beach in Northern California. One year later they were married. Their union has survived the rearing of two children, a handful of earthquakes registering over 6.5, numerous cats and a few special dogs, the latest of which is a yellow Lab named Annie Rose. Alice and her husband now live in a small rural town in Oregon, where she devotes the majority of her time to pursuing her second love, writing.

Alice loves to hear from readers. You can write her at P.O. Box 755, Brownsville, OR 97327. SASE for reply is appreciated.

Books by Alice Sharpe

CAST OF CHARACTERS

Brady Skye—The oldest son of alcoholic parents, this ex-cop has lost both the career and the woman he loves. Now someone's out to take something even more precious—but they'll have to kill Brady first.

Lara Kirk—Brokenhearted, she left when Brady rejected her. Now she's back with a secret capable of destroying them all.

Tom James—Will Brady's old partner let his temper be the death of him?

Chief Dixon—The chief's decades-long hatred of Brady's father has now spilled over onto Brady.

Billy Armstrong—Brady is almost positive the boy drew a gun. Most think it never existed. Billy's death throws Brady's and Lara's lives into a tailspin.

Bill Armstrong—Billy's father's lust for revenge is pushing him over the edge of sanity. He swears to ruin Brady as well as anyone Brady loves.

Jason Briggs—This teenager must be silenced.

Roberta Beaton—The querulous old woman will pay a price for her curiosity.

Karen Wylie—A rebellious teenager with dreams of becoming a movie star.

Nicole Stevens—She's positive something horrible has happened to Karen Wylie. And she may know what.

Charles Skye—Brady's father has been lost in a bottle for thirty years.

Garrett Skye—Brady's younger brother has become a bodyguard for a casino comptroller and his attorney wife. This decision to make more money so he can gain custody of his toddler daughter is about to blow up in his face.

Prologue

Officer Brady Skye scanned the dark, empty road. Parked on a side street, he waited for his shift to end, using the dashboard light to attend to last-minute paperwork. He checked his watch—a quarter of midnight and still hot outside. Well, that was August for you.

He checked his watch again a minute later and smiled at himself. Talk about being anxious. But in fifteen minutes, he'd be off duty for two weeks and in fifteen hours, he'd stand at the altar with Lara Kirk.

Again.

He had to admit he'd been confused when Lara suggested they elope a week before the wedding. Why would she want to ruin her big day?

Her smile had been wistful when she replied, *"My big day? You mean my mother's big day. This wedding is turning into the social event of the year, Brady, it's not about you and me anymore. I want to go to a justice of the peace. I want to get married, just the two of us, the way we wanted. Then we'll come back and do it Mom's way."*

The memory of that private, secret ceremony and the night that followed made Brady all the more anxious to put this shift to bed. He would make her the happiest woman in the world. Things would be perfect. He'd make them perfect.

The squad car radio burst into life at that moment. Brady leaned forward, adjusting the volume. He caught little more than *blue sedan, dented right front fender* before a car matching the description sped past. He reported his location and that he had the vehicle in sight, rattling off the license-plate number as he trailed behind.

Apparently noticing Brady's flashing lights, the sedan accelerated. It made a series of turns, brake lights flashing through intersections. Brady followed, but not too close. They weren't going to get very far and he didn't want to push them into doing something stupid.

More information came in over the radio as the sedan made a wide turn toward the river. *Car stolen, two suspects, both minors, unarmed, alleged to have lifted beer from the all-night store up on Breezeway...*

Brady and his brother, Garrett, had grown up in Riverport, Oregon, not far from this very neighborhood. Unless the kid driving that sedan had a trick up his sleeve, he'd soon dead-end against the gate securing the old Evergreen Timber loading dock.

But the gate was old, the chain connecting the two sides weak with rust. With barely a pause, the sedan busted through the gate and kept going, careening back and forth as it skidded toward the waterfront and the Columbia River beyond.

Dumb kids. Lifting a couple of cases of beer was nothing to die for, even if they'd compounded the offense by stealing a car. Brady backed off as his buddy and soon-to-be best man, Tom James, chimed in he was seconds away from lending backup.

A collision with a stack of oil drums saved the car from plunging into the river. With a series of thuds, the sedan came to a grinding halt in the middle of the pile, heavy drums rolling and bumping into each other with dull heavy clunks. An overhead light illuminated the scene. Brady stopped his car and exited, rushing forward as the welcome sound of a waning siren announced Tom's arrival.

A few empty beer cans fell to the ground as the driver and passenger doors opened. Two kids got out of the car. The passenger looked familiar, hardly unusual given Riverport's modest population of under five thousand. The driver, closest to Brady, stumbled once before taking off across the torn concrete, leaping over oil drums with surprising agility.

"Hey," Brady yelled as he pursued the driver, leaving the passenger to Tom who he'd heard come up behind him. Within a hundred yards, Brady caught up with the kid and wrestled him to the ground. He avoided a few drunken punches and a torrent of swearwords as he flipped him onto his stomach and cuffed him. He pulled the boy to his feet and marched him back to the squad car where he found no sign of Tom or the passenger.

"If you're smart, this will be the last night you ever get drunk," Brady said.

The kid swore at him again.

Once the driver was safely secured in the backseat, Brady turned his attention to Tom and the other teen, following their raised voices. The ground became trickier as the pool of light dispersed. Rambling blackberry vines had sprung up between the cracked concrete pads and snagged his pants as he ran. He got out his flashlight and flicked it on.

A movement caught Brady's eye. Two figures, six or seven feet apart, facing each other a scant foot or so from the edge of the wharf, the river a shimmering ribbon behind them. Tom, a barrel-chested man who had played football when young, was heaving after the run. He'd lost his hat in the chase and his balding dome glistened with sweat. The boy, only half Tom's size, appeared posed for flight. The kid yelled something was his fault as Tom's low voice droned on.

Brady hung back, giving Tom a chance to calm the kid with his usual aplomb. He had a way with kids though some in the department thought him too lenient. Nevertheless, Tom usually got his point across. The kid grew quiet. Good old Tom and his silver tongue.

Brady swung his flashlight down before switching it off. In the last instant before the beam died, he caught a glimpse of the boy reaching behind his back, his pale arm stark against his dark T-shirt, then the glint of light off metal as a gun emerged from beneath the shirt. It all happened in slow motion, time suspended—

A torrent of training flooded Brady's brain as he pulled his Glock. Tom was a microsecond away from taking a bullet in the gut and he obviously didn't know it. In that instant, Brady, without options, fired.

For a few seconds, the echo of the gunshot was the only sound in the world. The kid, bathed in shadows, flew to the ground.

The shot thundered again and again in Brady's head. He couldn't feel his hand still gripped around his gun. He saw Tom kneel beside the boy, his body mercifully blocking Brady's view for a brief moment, saw Tom's jaw work as he looked over his shoulder and yelled something, saw him yank his cell phone from his pocket and start punching in numbers.

The place would be swarming with help within minutes.

Brady, finally able to move, walked toward Tom and the still shape of the fallen boy. He'd lost his flashlight, he couldn't feel his feet, he still held the gun and it weighed a million pounds. He stopped short.

Tom's flashlight illuminated the scene. His florid face had taken on green undertones. "It's the Armstrong boy," he said. "He's dead."

Brady's heart sank like a rock to the very bottom of the sea. No wonder the kid had looked familiar. The Armstrong family had lost their only other child, a sixteen-year-old girl, a few weeks before. This kid was a year behind her in school. Billy, that was his name. Brady had gone to school with Bill Armstrong Senior.

His voice low as though afraid of being overheard, Tom said, "What in the hell happened?"

"He was going to shoot you," Brady said. *Wasn't it obvious?*

Tom shone a light at Billy's empty hands, flung toward the river. The boy's silver watchband shimmered on his wrist. "With what?"

Brady made himself concentrate past the roaring inside his head. "He pulled a gun out of his waistband in the back. There wasn't time to do anything but react."

"Are you sure? I mean, the light is tricky—"

"He pulled a gun." Brady tried to muster more confidence than he felt. He had seen a gun, hadn't he? *Oh, God...*

Tom's voice sounded just as dazed. "I was trying to talk some sense into him. You must have heard him, ranting and raving, blaming himself for his sister's suicide, blaming the cops—"

"I thought you had him calmed down, but when I lowered my flashlight, I saw him reach—"

"All right, Brady, all right. If you say there was a gun, there was a gun."

Brady wasn't any more convinced by Tom's words than by his own thoughts. If there'd been a gun, where was it now? If he'd made a mistake, how would he ever live with himself?

Tom pushed his hat back on his high forehead and added, "This is going to hit his parents hard. And Chief Dixon. A thing like this looks bad for the department and he's been waiting for you to mess up."

Like my father, Brady thought. He couldn't wrap his mind around any of that, not now, not so soon. Distant sirens announced the imminent arrival of the troops. The supervisor, an ambulance, the M.E. The place would soon be crawling with professionals.

"Lara, too," Tom added as though it just occurred to him. "I bet she got to know Billy and Sara down at the teen center."

Brady shook his head. He couldn't think. Wait, sure, she'd mentioned these kids along with a dozen others…

Tom suddenly seemed to grasp the impact of his comments. He said, "Damn, I'm sorry, Brady. Don't worry, if there was a gun, we'll find it. You saved my life. I won't forget it."

Brady's gaze shifted to the river rushing only a few feet from where the boy had fallen. If Billy Armstrong's gun had flown into the water as Billy took the bullet, it was possible they would never find it.

And in the back of his mind, a voice. Slurred like his

father's voice, thick with booze. *What if there wasn't a gun, you moron? What if you gunned down an unarmed kid? What then?*

Chapter One

One year later

The minute Lara drove over the bridge into Riverport, she knew coming back was a big mistake. It didn't matter how many times she told herself it was only for a couple of days, the feeling persisted. There was too much history here.

She turned on Ferry Street, passing the teen center without looking at it. Next came the bank and the hardware store. A red light at the corner of Ferry and Oak caught her as it always had. She kept her eyes on the road until the light turned green.

Her mother's big old Victorian sat perched on an acre of manicured gardens on the outskirts of town. Most of Riverport's other big old houses were gone, their land cut up and sold off to contractors for subdivisions. The mansion had been updated over the years—a solarium on the back, the kitchen expanded—until now it was quite a showpiece.

Lara had grown up in the house and it was with a surge of familiarity, if not homecoming, that she turned into the driveway. Her mother wasn't actually in residence as she'd left for an Alaskan cruise just a few days before. Myra, her mother's housekeeper, must have been waiting, though, for Lara had barely set the parking brake when the garage door rolled upward. Lara restarted the car and drove into the enclosure, sighing with relief when the doors closed behind her. She glanced into the backseat, then heard Myra coming through the side door that connected the house with the garage.

"Miss Lara," Myra called as Lara got out of the car. She approached with a big smile. "Your poor mother will just die when she learns she missed your visit. Here, let me help you."

Myra Halifax had worked for Lara's mother forever. A woman in her sixties with gray permed curls, she was built with a low center of gravity and formidable forbearance. That trait was a plus when it came to dealing with Lara's high-strung mother.

Lara returned the smile. She couldn't return the sentiment.

An hour later, she'd emptied the car and spent several moments upstairs settling into her old bedroom. Restless and uneasy, she decided something cold to drink and a friendly chat with the housekeeper might ward off her growing sense of foreboding.

She was one step into the kitchen when the doorbell rang. The shrill interruption came as a surprise. With her mother gone and her own presence in Riverport more or less a secret, company was unexpected and unwanted.

"I'll send whoever it is away," Myra said as she bustled past Lara into the foyer.

Lara hung back. There was a sense of destiny in the air, of colliding worlds. An overwhelming desire to race out the back swept through her and yet she stood off to the side as Myra impatiently flung open the door.

"You!" Myra said, and even though Lara couldn't see who stood on the front-porch step, she *knew*. Myra added, "What do you want?"

There was a pause during which Lara stopped breathing. Her heartbeat drummed in her head.

And then his voice.

"I need to speak to Mrs. Kirk."

"Mrs. Kirk is away for several weeks." Myra started to close the door.

Lara saw the hand that caught it. *His hand.* "Maybe you can help me."

Myra sputtered a little before saying, "I don't see how—"

"I need to get in touch with Lara," he cut in. "I have to talk to her. Warn her. All I need is her address or a telephone number."

Was it possible he didn't know she was at this house? It seemed so unlikely. No, someone must have seen her drive by, someone must have alerted him.

What else had they reported?

"I won't give you her phone number," Myra announced. "You broke her heart once and I won't stand by while you do it again."

Lara grabbed the edge of the door and opened it wider. "It's okay," she told Myra who stood her ground, glowering at their guest. Staring up into two very dark eyes, she added, "Hello, Brady."

For a second he didn't answer. For a second he looked as dumbstruck as she felt and she knew in that instant that he hadn't expected to find her here, that she was as much a surprise to him as he was to her.

That moment gave her a second to absorb his changed appearance. The thinner face, the longer hair, the hollows in his cheeks, the deep, deep tan, the solid muscles under the worn T-shirt, the dusty-looking jeans. What had happened to Mr. Press and Fold, Mr. Perfect Haircut, Mr. By the Book?

This Brady looked younger, rangier, cagier, sexier.

"I'm glad you're here," she said, which was an out-and-out lie. Sure, she'd planned on seeing him while she was in Riverport, of course, but not quite so soon, and not here at her mother's house. She'd spent three long hours in the car rehearsing her what-comes-next speech and now drew a total blank.

She hadn't taken one factor into account. She hadn't considered the impact of seeing him face-to-face. The months of tears that had cleared her head apparently hadn't cleared her heart. Yet.

"I'll just be a minute or two, Myra," she said with a backward glance. "You'll take care—"

"Of course," Myra huffed as Lara stepped onto her mother's broad porch and softly closed the door behind her.

"I was going to call you later," she told Brady.

Before he could answer, a car drove by, slowing down as the driver craned his neck to see who stood outside the Kirk house. Brady said, "Let's walk around back so we don't give the whole town something to talk about."

Lara suspected it was too late for that. She'd recognized Frank Duncan leaning forward, eyes wide. The hardware store would be abuzz within minutes. But she led the way around the back just the same, toward the riverside garden where they couldn't be overheard through the open windows.

The back sloped down to the river, which flowed by at a leisurely pace this late in the summer. Lara stopped by a grouping of wrought-iron patio furniture arranged on a brick island, surrounded by a sea of flowers. Too nervous to sit, she stood in back of a heavily scrolled chair, gripping the metal for support. Brady leaned against the edge of the old brick barbecue, linking his arms across his chest. He'd always been fit, but had his shoulders and arms always bulged with so many muscles?

"I didn't know you were in Riverport," he said.

"I've been here less than an hour." She tried not to stare at him but her traitorous gaze strayed his way every chance it got.

"How have you been?" he said.

She shook her head, unable to bear the thought of small talk.

"You look good," he added, his gaze taking her in from head to toe. She hadn't changed out of her traveling clothes, the white shorts and white halter top felt suddenly too revealing.

She whispered, "It's too late, Brady. I didn't come back for this."

His eyes flashed, then he smiled, kind of, his lips doing all the work, his eyes not playing along. "Oh? Then why did you come back? Explain it to me."

"Don't use that tone with me. You're the one who called everything off."

"And you're the one who left."

"You sent me packing like a kid. I was hurt at first but I'm over it now."

No reaction showed on his face. He was quiet for a long moment before saying, "Listen, Lara. Things between us ended kind of abruptly."

She met his gaze.

"Okay, okay, it's all my fault. I know that." He threw up both hands. "I admit it. I take full responsibility. I couldn't give you a whole man—"

"So you gave me nothing," she said, pushing herself away from the chair and walking toward the river and the abandoned dock her father had built twenty years before.

"I was a wreck—" he said from right behind her.

She jumped at the nearness of his voice. "Of course you were," she said, memories of the night flooding back. His stunned expression, his self-incrimination, the reality of the last few hours circling them like a cyclone, lifting them off their feet, tossing them around before flinging them back to earth a hundred miles from where they'd been.

She pushed it all away. "This is pointless. Let's skip the postmortem on our very short marriage. You told Myra you needed to warn me. Warn me about what?"

His voice, pitched low and combined with the mysterious intensity of his dark gaze, made Lara's knees go weak as he said, "I expected divorce papers by now."

"I have a lawyer working on them."

"For a year?"

"I haven't wanted anyone to know—"

"'Anyone' being your mother."

"Does it matter? I'm sorry I haven't moved fast enough for you. I'll get to it right away." The truth was the papers were ready. They were upstairs, in her suitcase. But she couldn't give them to Brady without an explanation. There were things he needed to know, things they needed to work out. But not now, not in her mother's garden, not when she needed to get back inside the house.

"The only reason it matters is Bill Armstrong," Brady said.

"Billy's father? Why—"

"Since the internal investigation found reasonable cause for the shooting, he's threatening a civil suit against me. I guess I don't blame him."

She waited.

With a bitter twist to his lips, he added, "They never found the gun and trust me, they looked. Armstrong insists his boy didn't have access to a handgun and wouldn't have carried one if he did. I still swear I saw one. It's a stalemate."

"But the river…" she began, something more niggling at the back of her mind. But what?

"Yeah. I know. It could be buried in three feet of silt and muck, it could be halfway to the ocean by now. Who knows?"

"Mr. Armstrong won't win."

"He'll have the sympathy of the jury. He lost both his kids within a month. And you know what the name Skye is worth around here."

"You are not your father," she said. She'd said it before, but it never seemed to sink in.

His laugh was sudden and without mirth. "You've always been naive. Maybe it comes from being born with a silver spoon in your mouth."

"And you've been afraid you'll turn into your father. It's not written that you will be a drunk and a loser."

"Ah, darling, it's the family tradition," he said, his voice low and silky and taunting. "My dad, my brother—"

I will not rise to the bait, she told herself and stood there with her mouth closed.

He finally added, "Anyway, it's not me I'm worried about."

"Maybe you should."

Frowning, he said, "What does that mean?"

"What's happened to you? When did you stop caring?"

"Stop caring about what? What are you talking about?"

"Your appearance, for instance. I can't believe the department lets you wear your hair that long."

"I'm not a policeman anymore, Lara. That part of my life is over. I thought you knew that."

She could hardly fathom such a thing. Brady had always wanted to be a cop. "Then what do you do?"

"I work construction like I did in college."

That explained the muscles. "But you were exonerated, weren't you? Why didn't you go back? Was it Chief Dixon?"

He shrugged and looked away.

"Brady," she said, touching his wrist. Big mistake. Sensory recognition traveled through her system like a lightning bolt, erasing the last three hundred sixty-three days in the blink of an eye. She drew her hand away at once. "You wouldn't have shot the boy if you hadn't had to," she said, her voice gentle. "You saved Tom's life."

He looked straight into her eyes and her heart quivered in her chest. She did not want to feel anything for him, let alone the tumultuous combination of lost love and resentment currently ricocheting inside her body like a wild bullet. Her mother had warned her a man with Brady's past could never really love anyone. Lara hadn't believed it until that night when he'd proved it to her.

He said, "I have nothing to lose. But you do."

"Me? Oh, you mean money. You think Bill Armstrong is going to come after my family's money."

"If he finds you're legally my wife, yes. If he finds a way to stick it to me or anyone I care—cared—about, yes, I do. Our marriage is a matter of public record. All he has to do is look. Maybe you ought to light a fire under your lawyer."

She closed her eyes, trying to imagine her mother's reaction to someone suing Brady and walking off with the Kirk fortune.

"It's not the civil suit I'm worried about," Brady added. "It's Armstrong himself. He's gone half-crazy since losing Billy. If he finds out about you—"

"Why would he even think about me?" she said, looking at Brady again, but her mind's eye casting a different image. Both of the Armstrong kids had come into the teen center on occasion. First Sara, Billy's delicate sixteen-year-old sister, then Billy and his pal, Jason Briggs, both a year younger. When Sara took a whole bottle of her grandmother's sleeping pills, it had stunned the community and it had devastated Billy.

The senior Armstrong had come into the teen center looking for answers no one could give him. Grief and anger had battled in his feverish eyes and she'd felt horrible for him. And truth be known, a little afraid of him, too.

And then, three weeks later, Billy died.

Good Lord, no wonder Brady looked haunted.

But she couldn't offer him what he needed. Maybe another woman could, someday, one who knew how to crack through his defenses or live with them. But not her. She said, "I've been gone a year, Brady. I'll leave again in a few days. As far as anybody in Riverport knows, I'm just the girl you didn't marry."

He looked down at his feet then back at her, his gaze unfathomable. How could she have ever thought she knew him better than she knew herself? He was a stranger. She glanced at her watch. Almost three o'clock. "I have to get back inside."

His eyebrows raised in query. Before he could ask a question she wasn't prepared to answer, she told him something she hadn't planned to. "I have a meeting this evening with Jason Briggs."

As she'd known it would, this news diverted his curiosity. "What does *he* want?"

"I guess he wants to talk."

"Why does the boy who convinced Billy Armstrong that stealing a car and a half case of beer was a good idea want to talk to you?"

She shrugged. "He got out of juvenile detention earlier this week and apparently went straight to the teen center. My replacement called me up in Seattle where I live now, and I called Jason. He asked if I was going to be around Riverport soon because he needed to talk."

"And so you drove all the way back here to talk with a delinquent sixteen-year-old boy."

"Among other things," she hedged. "But, yes. There was something in his voice."

"What do you mean?"

"He sounded nervous."

"Jason Briggs hasn't, to my knowledge, told anyone anything about that night except to try to blame everything on Billy."

She almost smiled. Brady was acting like what

Brady really was. A cop. How could he not see that? She said, "I won't know what's troubling him until I talk to him."

"Yeah. Okay, I'll go with you. This may be a break."

"No, you won't go with me," she said firmly.

"Where are you meeting him?"

"Like I'm going to tell you?"

"You don't know what he has in mind."

"And neither do you," she said. With a warning glance, she added, "Come back later tonight. If Jason says anything I can pass along to you, I will."

"I don't like you going alone."

She stared at him until he had the grace to drop his gaze. "I'll call my lawyer tomorrow. We'll have this sham of a marriage annulled."

One minute he was staring at her as she talked and the next he'd closed the three feet between them and grabbed her arms. The energy that surged directly into her bloodstream almost knocked her off her feet. Her heart banged against her ribs.

He dipped his head so low his deep dark brown eyes burned into hers. "Can a marriage consummated the way ours was *be* annulled?"

"Brady…"

"Don't you remember our wedding night? Don't you remember what we did—"

She shrugged herself away from him. Sex had never been the issue. "You'd better go now."

Seconds ticked by in absolute silence before he finally moved. He paused at her elbow. "I'll be back at nine o'clock."

"Make it ten," she said.

He nodded once before striding away. She stood in

the garden for several moments, staring out at the old dock, waiting until she heard the roar of his motorcycle and knew it was safe to move.

Then she walked back inside the house, head high, eyes mostly unseeing. She'd shed her last tear for Brady months before. She was over him.

Chapter Two

Good Neighbors was a nonprofit organization utilizing volunteer workers to build low-income housing. Brady was one of the few paid employees. It was his job to assign and approve projects. He was also in charge of contracting jobs too big for the volunteers to handle alone.

The man who had donated the property had been truly generous as it wasn't a tiny city lot but a small parcel backed by the river. Eventually there would be additional houses built on the property. Brady hoped to have a hand in all of them.

After visiting with Lara, Brady couldn't keep his mind on anything. The sun baked his bare back as he sat on the plywood roof, banging in a slew of nails. They'd run out of ammo for the nail gun and he'd sent everyone else home for the day.

Had Lara really come back to Riverport just to talk to Jason Briggs? What was the boy up to? He'd been in and out of trouble most of his young life and Brady would bet money a few months in detention hadn't changed that. Brady knew the type, his own brother, Garrett, was a carbon copy.

For a second, Brady thought about Garrett and wondered where he lived now and what he was up to. Last he'd heard, Garrett was out of the army. Brady hoped that gig had helped his little brother get his head screwed on straight, but he wouldn't count on it. Garrett was more like their father than Brady was. The same reckless streak ran through both of them.

A bitter smile never touched his lips as that thought hit home. Could Garrett have done any worse with his life than Brady had? Had he killed a fifteen-year-old boy? Had he destroyed his one chance for a happy marriage with a woman who outclassed him in every way possible? Had he abandoned the only job he ever truly wanted and cemented his reputation as another worthless Skye, all because the thought of carrying a gun—and possibly making another mistake—made him queasy?

Unless Garrett had turned into a serial killer, he was probably doing as well if not better than his responsible big brother.

Brady missed a nail head twice and laid the hammer aside. Staring out at the river, he faced the fact he wasn't going to get much more done here today. He picked up his tools and scrambled down the ladder. He'd just finished storing the equipment in the on-site storage shed when an SUV pulled up alongside his Harley.

Brady yanked on his T-shirt as the dust settled around the SUV. The window slid down to reveal Tom James, flush face toying with a smile.

Twice divorced, Tom was five or six years older than Brady, creeping up on forty. His former partner was also shorter than Brady, heavier, big chested with very short black hair ringing a bald spot.

"Have I got news for you," Tom said.

Brady leaned against Tom's vehicle. It was brand new and the fact he could afford it after the cleaning his last ex-wife and her lawyer accomplished, spoke to the fact that Tom was banking on his future promotion within the Riverport Police Department.

And no reason he shouldn't. Brady was just damn thankful the Armstrong shooting hadn't destroyed Tom's reputation on the force as well as his own.

"Let me guess," Brady said.

Tom laughed. "You won't guess this. I got it hot from Carlson's Hardware Store."

"Lara is back in town, staying at her mother's house while her mother is on a cruise."

Tom's round face fell. "Someone told you."

"I saw Lara. I spoke with her."

Tom nodded, all humor gone now. He knew what the last year had cost Brady. He said, "How was it?"

"About how you'd expect."

Tom nodded. "What did she come back for?"

"She's meeting Jason Briggs tonight."

"Really," Tom said, eyes narrowing. "I heard he got out of juvie. What's she meeting him for?"

"He wanted to talk to her. Maybe you could keep your eyes open tonight just in case there's trouble."

"Where are they meeting? What time?"

"Don't know, she won't say."

"You going to tail her?"

Brady shook his head. "She'd kill me if she found out I was butting into her business."

"So?"

"So, she's right."

"But you want me to keep an eye out," Tom said, a smile pulling at his lips.

Brady looked away.

"Don't worry, buddy, I'll mention it to Chief Dixon, too. He can tell anyone else he sees fit."

Brady bit his tongue at this suggestion but said nothing as Tom drove off. He just hoped Lara never got wind that half the Riverport police force would soon know—thanks to him—that she had a meeting with Jason Briggs.

The thought occurred to Brady as he climbed on the Harley that Jason's driver's license had been yanked. Using a little deduction, that meant Lara would probably meet him in town. Like maybe at the teen center or the diner or even Lara's mother's house. He toyed with doing a little research but let the idea go.

Lara had made it clear she didn't want him in her face. Tom was going to keep a sharp eye peeled just in case. That was enough.

He got to his place about five o'clock and ate a tuna sandwich while standing at the counter. It was a new place, about as nondescript as they come. He'd changed just about everything in the last year, including his residence. The old place had reminded him too much of Lara.

At first, after the shooting, he'd toyed around with leaving Riverport himself. Without his job on the force, without Lara, what was there to stay for? But then the Good Neighbors job came along and he admitted to himself that, for good or bad, Riverport was home. Garrett could move around the country all he wanted— Brady would stay here.

After dinner, he usually went back to the Good Neighbors house to map out the next day's activities. No reason not to do so again tonight. He couldn't sit in the impersonal apartment longing for a life he no longer had. He was too restless to read or watch television. If he couldn't settle down at work, he'd take the Harley out to the river and use an evening swim to work out his anxiety.

He and Lara used to do that, most of the time on the spur of the moment after a movie or dinner out. He could still picture her in the scraps of satin and lace she called underwear, swimming in the river, honey-blond hair mingling with the darkening water, the summer smell of blackberries, the taste of her skin. She wore summer the way some women wore diamonds...

He'd go anyway. Despite all that.

It took him two hours to plan the next day's work and finish up a few odd jobs. It was nearing nine o'clock by the time he started home. He went the long way in order to avoid the Kirk house. He wasn't due there for over an hour and he didn't want Lara catching sight of him and accusing him of spying.

He was driving down Main Street near the west end of town, undecided about the swim, when he spotted Tom talking to what appeared to be a high-school girl standing beside a little blue car. She'd probably been caught speeding. As usual, when Tom put on the charm, a scared kid relaxed. Brady knew he wouldn't give her a ticket, he'd cut her some slack. Back in the day, Brady had actually talked to Tom about his live-and-let-live take on citing minors, questioning whether he was actually doing a kid much good by not holding them accountable for minor offenses. Tom had laughed him off.

And again, that ache of no longer belonging. He missed being out on the street, helping people, looking for miscreants, figuring things out. Sure, he was still alive, he still walked and talked and worked and occasionally, even laughed. But it all seemed brittle and hollow. His life, abandoned.

Not wanting to talk to Tom again, he took a side street that led to the industrial side of town. There was a smattering of bars along the street. No doubt his father was holding up a stool at the River Rat or the Crosshairs. Brady avoided even looking in the open doors.

That's when he caught sight of a guy on a bicycle who looked familiar. Of course. Hair shorter, body a little bigger, but that was Jason Briggs.

For one long second, options flashed through Brady's mind. Turn around and go the other way, pull over to the curb, find a cold drink and do nothing or…

Brady slowed way down, giving Jason a good lead. He waited until Jason had cleared the edge of town and disappeared around a corner before taking off, hanging back, trailing him but not close.

What was the harm of trailing Jason if Lara never knew?

It looked as though the kid was headed for the river. Maybe he just wanted a swim. Maybe Brady would join him—if Lara wasn't there. Who knows what Jason might talk about while paddling around the river on a summer evening?

Traffic was light, so following Jason took skill. Brady left lots of room between them, uneasy with the inevitable times Jason disappeared around a curve. But Brady knew this road and there was only one place it really went—to the river. Unless the kid was headed over the bridge and on up to St. George.

Brady came around the latest hairpin curve to find

the road ahead empty. This was where it branched, straight across the bridge, or an abrupt right on the south side of the river. The bridge had two cars on it but no bikes. That left the southern road and it appeared empty. Brady concluded Jason had ridden his bike into the turnout on this side of the bridge.

So, he wasn't going to swim. The bank there was too steep, the river too deep thanks to the proximity of the bridge excavation. There was a far better spot just a quarter of a mile downstream where the river made a wide turn.

As the noisy motorcycle would ruin a stealthy approach, Brady steered the Harley behind a few trees, took off his helmet and started walking.

He found Jason still astride his bike, feet planted on the ground, facing the road. Waiting. He was wearing earphones attached to an iPod in his pocket. He was a lanky, fair-haired kid with shifty eyes, dressed in baggy shorts and flip-flops. Brady remembered the punches he'd thrown the night of the shooting, and his own advice to Jason: stop drinking. Well, they didn't serve adult beverages in juvenile detention, so hopefully a little time away from temptation had been good for him.

Brady ducked behind some very dense Oregon grape bushes. He scooted along until an abandoned wooden pavilion provided cover from the road and the parking area. The downside of this position was he couldn't see the road. The upside was twofold—he could, by contorting a bit, see the clearing and no one could see him.

Ten long minutes later, he heard an engine. Jason must have seen a car. He took off the earphones and got off his bike, pushing it near a picnic table where he leaned it against one of the benches. At last, a silver car with Washington plates drove slowly into the clearing.

Brady saw Lara behind the wheel. She parked the car facing the river embankment and rolled down her window. Jason walked toward Lara with his head down.

Brady tensed. He could imagine no reason Jason Briggs would hurt Lara, but his walking up to her like that made him nervous.

They spoke for a few seconds and Jason started around the back of the car. Lara's window slid back into place. Had she seen the Harley? Was she going to drive Jason to a different spot?

But Jason got inside the car and turned in the seat to face Lara. Brady could tell she hadn't turned the engine off. Probably wanted to keep the air-conditioning running.

He watched them talk for a couple of minutes, then became aware of an idling engine out on the road. Before he could finish wondering what Lara and Jason would do when another car rolled into the parking lot, a shot blasted the evening stillness.

An instant later, a muffled scream hit Brady like a gust from a tornado. It came from Lara's car. There was a perfect round hole in her back window. Jason had slumped forward. Lara leaned toward him. Brady started moving. Another shot. Some idiot was out on the road, shooting at Lara's car.

Before he could scramble from behind the pavilion, Lara put the car into gear and gunned the engine into a broad turn to escape. It appeared Jason fell against her during the turn. Another shot. She grabbed her arm. The car lurched forward. Brady watched helplessly as it hung on the embankment for a second before heading for the river.

As he ran toward the quickly disappearing car, he

heard an engine rev and tires squeal out on the road. No doubt thinking his mission accomplished, the gunman had fled. Every cop-related fiber of Brady's body quaked at the thought of the gunman getting away.

He got to the embankment in time to see Lara's car fly over a strip of boulders, its tailpipe clanging as the car launched into the river, a geyser of water spraying as it landed like a whale doing a belly flop, and quickly sank from view.

Chapter Three

Jason's limp body pinned Lara's foot against the accelerator pedal. Blood from the wound on her right arm dripped on his white T-shirt as she tried to push him away.

Oh, God, he was hurt, she didn't want to hurt him further, but the car was racing toward the river.

A final push and he slumped the other direction. She moved her foot and the racing engine slowed, but it was too late. The car hit the rocks skirting the river's edge and launched itself into the water. Her last act before she hit the river was to pound the electric window button. The window slid down six inches before water washed over the hood and the engine died. Within an instant, water covered the windshield and the vehicle sank to the bottom of the river as cold water gushed through the window.

"Jason!" she screamed.

He mumbled something as the water seemed to revive him for a moment. It was too dark to see much. "Jason, we're sinking. I'm going to try to get us out of this. Hold on."

A million images flashed through her mind as she

searched frantically for something heavy enough to break a window. *Her purse, no. Sandals, a small flashlight. Nothing heavy. No big tire iron.*

A million images. Brady. Nathan. Her mother. A million regrets, a million sorrows, all racing like electronic bleeps through her brain, like a movie reel moving too fast for images. And all the while she searched for a tool that would break the window and save their lives, and all the time she searched, she knew no such tool existed within the passenger cabin of her new car.

The water was up to their waists now and still gushing. She wished she'd not lowered the window or had thought to do it sooner though twin streams also spurt from the bullet holes in the back window. Her actions had more or less set them up for certain death. No one knew they were there but the person who shot them. He or she wasn't coming to their rescue.

She should have told Brady! She should have told her mother's housekeeper. She should have told someone.

How long would it take for anyone to notice she was gone. Nathan would first, of course, and then Myra, but neither of them would tell the one person who could help.

Brady. She should have told Brady.

She held Jason's head up for him as he seemed to have slipped back into unconsciousness and the water was above her shoulders. He would die without the terror. Lucky him.

A banging on the window behind her head caused Lara to gulp river water and she coughed. A rock. Someone was using a big rock to pound on the rear window. She immediately shoved Jason through the middle of the car, between the two front seats into the back, the water making it easier to move him, struggling to keep his face up, his nose above water. He ran into the seat and sputtered as she lost hold of him. She felt around in a panic until she caught hold of his hair and hauled him back to the surface. He gagged. At least he was still alive.

There was only a small pocket of air against the ceiling of the car now. The rock pounding sounded hollow until suddenly the window shattered into a thousand little cubes of glass. Hands reached inside. She shoved Jason toward them, praying the car hadn't sunk too deep, that their savior would get Jason to the surface before he gulped too much water and drowned.

As Jason's feet disappeared, Lara pushed herself through the seats. Her sandal strap caught on the gearshift and she wasted precious seconds yanking it off her foot. Hands appeared again, reaching toward her. She reached out. They grabbed her. A feeling of safety shot through her body as the hands pulled her free of the car. Her rescuer put an arm around her waist and swam to the surface, towing her along.

She emerged into the warm night air coughing and choking. Arms lifted her from her feet and carried her up the steep embankment, laying her down on the grass beside Jason, who was being tended by an older woman Lara had never seen before. A gray car was parked a few feet away, the driver's door wide open. A beeping sound indicated the keys were still in the ignition.

Lara coughed up a half gallon of water before looking up at the man who had saved her.

Dripping wet, hair streaming down his brown face,

clothes molded against his powerful body, expression unfathomable.

Brady.

Somewhere in her heart of hearts, she'd known it was him. "Why are you here?" she sputtered.

"It's a long story," he said, leaving her side to kneel beside Jason. "This lady saw your car go into the river as she crossed the bridge. She called an ambulance on her cell phone." He put his fingers against Jason's throat. Even from where Lara sat, she could see the spreading red stain on Jason's chest and she groaned.

"His breathing is shallow, he's going into shock," Brady said. Addressing the Good Samaritan, he added, "Do you have a blanket in your car, something to keep him warm?"

"I'll look," she said, struggling to her feet.

"He's lost a lot of blood," Brady said as he propped the boy's feet atop a rock. Lara took Jason's limp hand. He felt so cold.

Brady was in the act of stripping off his wet T-shirt, when the woman hurried from her car carrying a blue blanket. He rung out his shirt before wadding it up and placing it on Jason's wound. The muscles under his wet skin rippled with effort.

"It's the dog throw," the flustered woman said as she pushed the blanket toward Brady. "It's probably hairy—"

"It's fine," Brady said, tucking the blanket around the wet boy. "Can you take over for me? Can you keep pressure on his wound?"

"Of course." The woman did as Brady asked before looking up at him with frightened eyes. "This is a gunshot, isn't it?"

"Yes."

"And the girl?"

Now that survival wasn't foremost on her mind, Lara realized she felt not only light-headed, but her arm throbbed. She looked down to find new blood seeping into the wet cloth, making a pink watercolor of her blouse.

Brady took her good hand, pulling her to her feet. She stumbled against him and he caught her, his grip tight.

"You okay?"

No, she wasn't okay. She wasn't okay at all. She'd come close to dying. She'd come close to leaving secrets untold. She had to bite back tears as she said, "You know about the shooting?"

"Yeah."

"I don't understand. How did you get here?"

"Put some pressure on your arm," he said evasively. "Better yet, keep it elevated." He looked toward the road. "I hear a siren. Let's hope they had the good sense to alert the police."

OVERLAID ON THE IMAGE of Jason's unconscious body being loaded into the ambulance as red and blue police lights flashed in the dark was the old replay of the same thing being done to Billy Armstrong.

Two boys out for a joyride. One dead, the other hovering near death.

And now Lara.

Along with the police, two ambulances had responded. The ambulance carrying Jason took off almost immediately. The other stood waiting for Lara. Brady watched as Lara greeted one of the EMT guys like an old, lost friend. They'd probably gone to school together. It struck Brady that Lara had walked away from her whole life—her family, her friends, her job—when she walked away from him.

Ran away. And what choice did you give her?

"I have to talk to you," she told him, pausing as a medic guided her to the ambulance.

"Did Jason have a chance to say anything to you?" he asked.

She cradled her wounded arm with her good hand. Sympathy, the last thing he wanted from her, flooded her eyes. She said, "He was just getting settled when it happened. The only person he had a chance to mention was his girlfriend, the Wylie girl. I guess she broke up with him."

"That's all?"

"Yeah. I'm sorry." She lowered her voice and added, "I need to talk to you about something even more important. I could have died tonight. I would have died if you hadn't magically appeared."

"Not magically," he said, gazing into her green eyes. The flashing lights cast revolving colors across her hair and face. Her eyes glistened.

So many memories. Of holding her, kissing her, making love to her. She had been his and he'd lost her.

"There's something I have to tell you," she repeated.

"Me, too. I didn't just happened to be here tonight."

She shook her head. "I don't care. I'll wait for you at the hospital. Come get me when you can."

"Just tell me now—"

"Not now," she said. He felt his throat close as she walked away. His last glimpse was of her eyes before the ambulance doors shut and the vehicle charged back to town.

Tom hadn't arrived yet, but his new partner, a young

guy named Hastings, took Brady's statement, russet eyebrows arching when Brady described the gunfire.

"Two shots," Brady said. "Maybe three."

"But you didn't see the vehicle?"

"No."

"Show me again where you were standing when the shots started."

Brady walked Hastings through the whole thing, using flashlights. Tow trucks had arrived and the underwater recovery of the vehicle had begun. Hastings left as another squad car tore into the clearing and Tom emerged, tugging on his hat. Hastings and Tom spoke for a few seconds, then Tom came to stand beside Brady.

"I'd like to get to the hospital," Brady said.

Tom nodded. "Soon. But hell, Brady, what were you doing out here? Did you follow Lara?"

"Actually, I followed Jason Briggs. I saw him riding his bike."

"You followed Jason? With what?"

"The Harley. It's parked down the road, behind some trees."

"Let me get this straight. You shadowed the kid out of town, then hid your motorcycle and continued on foot? Why?"

Brady shrugged. "Because the Harley is noisy and I didn't want Jason to know I was following him."

"He never saw you?"

"I don't think so."

"And when you got here—"

"I stayed out of sight."

"How long did he and Lara talk before the attack? Did he say anything about Billy having a gun?"

"He didn't have time. They only talked for a minute

or two. She said he never got past mentioning his girl-friend. A girl named Wylie."

"What about her?"

"I guess she broke up with Jason. You'll have to ask Lara."

"And you didn't see the gunman or his vehicle?"

"No."

"This doesn't look so good," Tom said, pushing his hat back on his head.

Brady's eyes narrowed as he said, "Just what are you suggesting, Tom?"

"Nothing. Nothing. But you've got to admit it looks bad."

"Why?"

"The first day you find out Jason Briggs is home you follow him. The next thing anyone knows, the boy is as good as dead. And you're on scene."

"Are you saying I shot Jason Briggs?"

"I'm saying it looks like you could have shot the boy. He was the only other one in the car with Billy Armstrong that night. He's fresh out of juvie. If he knew something maybe you didn't want him telling, he might confide in his old counselor—"

"I am this close to giving you a black eye," Brady growled, his fist bunched into a knot.

Tom shook his head. "I know you didn't do this, pal. No matter how you felt about Jason, you would never have jeopardized Lara. But Chief Dixon is going to ask these questions."

"I don't have anything against Jason. Did you tell Dixon about Jason wanting to talk to Lara?"

Tom thought for a second. "I guess so. At the briefing. Sure."

"And how many others?"

"I don't know. Half a dozen."

"Any way for Bill Armstrong to have heard the news?"

Tom thought again for a second before saying, "His ex-brother-in-law works in dispatch so I guess it's possible. What are you getting at?"

"I don't know what I'm getting at." Brady took a steadying breath. "How do we know Lara wasn't the real victim?"

"Why would anyone want to shoot her?"

"I don't know. Ask Bill Armstrong where he was tonight."

"Don't start on that. Bill Armstrong wouldn't shoot Jason Briggs."

"Wouldn't he? Your scenario of my not wanting Jason to tell Lara something might also pertain to Armstrong. Maybe there's something Billy told Jason that Armstrong doesn't want Jason telling Lara. Or maybe he just wants to hurt Lara to get back at me."

"Is something going on between you two?"

"No," Brady said. "But he doesn't know that."

Tom looked unconvinced. "We'll talk again tomorrow."

How DID YOU FIND a madman when you had no clues? Jason could have made new enemies in juvenile detention, he could have tempted old enemies who heard he was back in town and saw him riding his bike off on his own. Like Brady had. Was he sure there hadn't been a third party trailing him while he trailed Jason? Had he even thought to look?

No, and yet somehow Brady didn't believe that was

the answer. He thought it was as simple as someone not wanting Jason Briggs talking to Lara Kirk.

Why?

Or maybe someone wanted Lara dead and was a lousy shot.

Twenty minutes after leaving the clearing, he entered the emergency-room doors for the first time in almost a year, nodding at the nurse behind the desk as his still-soggy boots squeaked with every step. In lieu of a shirt, which he'd donated to help stem Jason's bleeding, he wore an old jacket he carried on the bike. It was too hot a garment for August.

"Hey, Brady. Long time no see."

"How you doing, Tammy? I'm here to check on Lara Kirk and Jason Briggs."

She frowned for a second. About his own age, she looked ten years older, probably because she smoked like a fiend when no one was watching. Brady had caught her outside a few times and used to tease her about it.

"Ms. Kirk was treated for a superficial gunshot wound in her right arm and was released an hour ago. The Briggs boy is in surgery. It's touch and go."

"I thought Ms. Kirk was going to wait for me," Brady mused aloud, unsure what to do now.

"She got a call and left."

Brady thanked her briskly and took off. Who had called her? Why? What was important enough for her to leave the hospital when she'd made a point of telling him to meet her there? Was it possible she didn't under-stand the importance of the fact that Jason Briggs wasn't the only one who had been shot tonight?

He got as far as the Harley before feeling a hulking

presence behind him. He turned abruptly and immediately recognized Bill Armstrong emerging from between parked cars.

Armstrong was about the same size as Brady though a couple of years older. He'd been a mechanic since graduating from high school. Married his high-school sweetheart. As far as Brady knew, he'd been doing okay for himself and his family until his daughter committed suicide and a few weeks later, his son died.

Thanks to Brady.

Now word was that Bill Armstrong had taken to drinking, his wife had threatened to leave him and his job was in peril.

"I heard you almost killed another kid tonight," Armstrong said, coming to a halt six feet away from Brady. The overhead lights illuminated the thatch of sandy hair that continued around his face in a trimmed beard.

"You heard wrong," Brady said. He didn't want to waste time with Armstrong, but he didn't want to turn his back on him, either.

"I heard Jason Briggs got shot and that you were there."

Brady waited.

"That little gal who left when you murdered my son is back in Riverport."

"Who told you that?"

He tapped his forehead with a finger. "I just know. Maybe it would have been better for her if she'd stayed away."

Brady advanced a few steps. "She was a counselor to your kids," he said. "She tried to help them. She's an innocent in all this."

Armstrong backed down a little. He looked in the direction of his shoes as he said, "Do you suppose she'd miss you if some concerned citizen took it in his mind to eliminate a public menace?"

Brady's gut tightened. His decision to stop carrying a gun suddenly seemed shortsighted.

"I don't, either," Armstrong said. "But killing you is too easy." His voice caught. "I want you to know what it's like to lose someone you love," Armstrong continued, his eyes moist now. "If you had a son it would be perfect. An eye for an eye. Poetic justice."

"Where were you tonight?" Brady said softly.

Ignoring the question, Armstrong said, "You don't know what it's like to lose a kid."

With total sincerity, Brady said, "I've told you a dozen times how sorry I am about your son. I had no choice. There was no time. He pulled a gun."

Please, God, let that be true…

For a second, Armstrong looked ready to throw his weight at Brady. And then he rocked back on his heels and steadied himself by grabbing the hood of the closest car.

Brady picked his helmet up off the seat. "Stay away from Lara Kirk and Jason Briggs," he said.

Armstrong shook his head. He took a deep breath and glared at Brady. "You're not a cop anymore, Skye. You're a washed-up has-been just like your old man. Maybe the other cops let you off the hook for murdering my kid, but I won't. You'll pay for what you did to me and mine."

"I know," Brady said. "You're going to take me for every dime I have."

The smile that broke Armstrong's face was worse than his sneer. "That'll be a start. We'll see where it ends."

Brady got on the bike and started the engine.

Was Armstrong a grieving man, more bark than bite, or was Brady's gut feeling Lara was in terrible danger more than his guilty conscience at work?

At any rate, he wasn't going to leave her alone tonight. He'd swing by his place and grab a toothbrush and some dry shoes and clothes. Trade the Harley for his truck in case they needed to go somewhere. Like it or not, she had a guard tonight.

WHAT WAS KEEPING Brady?

Lara stood by the front windows, freshly showered, wearing old sweats she'd found in a bottom drawer. She was still cold even though she knew it was a warm night, summer at its apex. When she closed her eyes, the cold river flooded her head.

Before the night was over she would tell Brady what she'd come back to Riverport to tell him.

She'd wanted to tell him forever.

The sitting room, as her mother called the room to the left of the foyer, was typical Victorian with very high ceilings and tall, stately windows. A rose and ivory Oriental carpet, its silk soft against Lara's bare feet, covered the hardwood floor.

"Lara?" Lara turned at the sound of the housekeeper's voice. "Everything is quiet upstairs," Myra added. "I think I'll turn in."

"Of course. Thanks for your help today. I don't know what I would have done without you."

"I wouldn't have missed it for the world. I'm just glad I didn't go on that cruise with your mother like she wanted. I did that once a couple of years ago and if you don't mind my saying, it wasn't much of a vacation for me."

Lara nodded. She could imagine. As Myra left the room, a pair of headlights pulled up in front of the house. Lara recognized Brady's green truck parked under the streetlight and she left the room, headed for the front door, suddenly aware her feet tingled and her palms felt sweaty. She took a deep breath as she pulled open the door.

He looked up as he took the last few steps. He'd obviously taken a shower and changed clothes and in the porch light, dressed in black jeans and a gray Henley, he looked lean, capable and focused.

She stood aside and he entered the house. He paused in the foyer, his gaze traveling up the broad, curved staircase as though looking for an invading army. Then his eyes met hers.

"You left the hospital."

"Myra called. She was having trouble—"

"What kind of trouble?" He covered the few steps between them and caught her arm. She recoiled and he dropped his hand.

"I'm sorry. I forgot about your wound."

"It's okay. There's a huge bandage on it. The doctor said there might be a scar but there was no permanent damage."

"Good. What kind of trouble did the housekeeper have?"

She looked away for a second, then back at him. "It didn't have anything to do with tonight, Brady, honest. I found a cab outside the hospital and took it home. Myra had to pay the man. I'd forgotten I no longer have a purse or a wallet. Do you know how Jason is doing?"

"I called from my place. He's out of surgery, but it's still touch and go."

She nodded. Touch and go. "Poor kid."

They each stared at the floor for a moment, then spoke at the same time.

She said, "Let's go sit down—"

And he said, "I'm staying here tonight—"

They both stopped talking, he turned his hand palm up as if to give her a turn first. She repeated herself. He sat down on the second from bottom step and patted the space next to him.

Lara understood that he felt uncomfortable in her mother's house and was reluctant to stray too far inside.

"You're nervous," he said.

She nodded.

"I want you to know I didn't follow you out to the river. You told me not to come, but I happened to see Jason riding his bike and—"

She put her hand on his arm and he met her eyes. "You saved my life. You saved Jason. How could you think I would resent you being there?"

"Well, you're nervous."

"Not about that."

"And you're angry with me."

"Oh, Brady. It's been a long year." Tears stung the back of her nose and she struggled to keep them out of her eyes and her voice. Though they didn't fall, the emotion behind them must have showed, because he covered her hand with his.

His face was very close. She could smell soap and aftershave and toothpaste. She stared at his lips. Flames licked her groin.

And just like that, their lips drifted together, inevitably, touching in a way that was at once familiar and bittersweet. These lips she'd thought she'd never touch again. Soft and warm with the power of life behind them.

But not for her. Not ever again.

She drew away and took a shaky breath.

"I'm sorry," he said.

"It's me. My emotions are all over the map."

"I won't let it happen again," he added. "I promise you."

She nodded.

"What do you want to tell me?" His hand had slipped from hers.

She bit her lip and finally decided how she should share her news. "Come with me," she said, standing. He stood as well and seemed startled when she led him up the stairs. Was he remembering the first time they'd climbed these stairs together, two and a half years ago when her mother had taken off for the Aegean Sea and Lara had used the opportunity to show him the room in which she'd grown up?

Things like that were impossible when her mom was in the house for the simple reason her mother didn't like Brady. She was one of those people Brady talked about, one of those who based their opinion of him on his family name. To Lara's mother, Brady was and always would be, "One of those worthless Skye boys." Slightly less troublesome than the younger boy, Garrett, but not to be trusted just the same.

She led Brady into her old bedroom. The light was low, the bed was covered in white eyelet just as it had been years before when she lived at home with her mother. Knowing she was coming, Myra had filled vases with roses from the garden and placed them around the room. Their fragrance perfumed the air.

"This is why I rushed home from the hospital," she said softly.

His brow furrowed as he looked at the bed, which suddenly seemed to glow with remembered passion. She moved aside so he could see what occupied the far corner.

So he could see the crib.

"Myra needed help getting Nathan to sleep," she said.

She watched his face as realization dawned. It was like watching the sunrise. He glanced at her and she nodded once, sniffing back tears before they could glisten in her eyes.

He moved toward the crib like a sleepwalker and stood staring down at the slumbering infant within.

Chapter Four

"He was conceived on our wedding night," Lara said. "His name is Nathan."

He had a son?

Just like that? One moment alone in the world, the next moment, a son?

Very slowly, he lowered his hand until the backs of his fingers grazed the baby's round cheek. How could skin be that soft? The baby tucked one tiny fist close to his chin. A bubble blew at his lips and then he made a sudden face, a frown, and scrunched up his tiny body before relaxing again, hands flung to the side.

His son. *Nathan.*

"You named him after your father," he whispered.

"Yes."

Brady kept his gaze glued to the infant because he didn't trust himself to look at Lara. Men usually had a few months to prepare themselves for fatherhood. Time to get used to the idea of a baby, to merge the dreamy possibilities of the future with the uncertainties of the past. Time to reckon.

But she'd deprived him of this.

She hadn't trusted him with the knowledge he was

to become a father. She'd gone through pregnancy and birth and the first three months of his child's life alone rather than trust him.

She's here now, a small voice whispered in the back of his mind. *They're both here now.*

He wasn't ready to listen. He shoved his hands in his pockets as he turned to face her.

Their eyes locked for a heartbeat before she lowered her gaze. "I'm sorry, Brady," she said so softly it might have been his imagination. "I was frightened."

That made it better? Now she not only didn't trust him and didn't like him, she was afraid of him?

"Later," he forced himself to say. He needed time to think.

"I just want you to know I didn't know I was pregnant when I first went away, and when I found out—"

He held up a hand to still her.

The baby made a little noise and Lara leaned over, her shoulder brushing Brady's arm. She grabbed her own arm, wincing, and he remembered her injury and how close he'd come to losing her. Good God, if she'd died tonight, would anyone have bothered to tell him about Nathan?

"Will you lift him for me?" she said, glancing up at him. "Or shall I call Myra?"

Brady blinked a time or two. "I can do it."

"It's easy, just make sure you support his head," she said.

And so he lifted his son for the first time, careful to put one hand behind the little guy's heavy head. The baby kicked and squirmed and Brady held on tight, terrified he'd drop him.

"Relax," Lara said. "You're doing fine."

"What do I do now?"

"Just comfort him, Brady. Hold him closer. Don't be afraid."

He pulled Nathan against his chest, one hand all but covering the small boy's back. He tried making soft noises and bouncing a little. One or the other of these tactics apparently worked because the baby settled down. Brady tipped him away from his chest for a moment, anxious to really look at these few pounds of humanity that had instantly redefined his life.

His throat tightened as he took in every amazing inch of his son's face. The dark orbs as he opened one eye, then the other. The very small nose, the tip of a tiny tongue. What struck him was the baby's total dependence. *Was he ready for this?*

He was still trying to work out his complicated relationship with his own father. What did he know about being a father to an innocent child? How could he teach what he'd never learned?

"Did you hear that?" Lara said, and he opened his eyes abruptly, yanked back from his thoughts.

"Did I hear what?"

"A noise downstairs. Maybe it was Myra."

"I'll go take a look," Brady said.

The door flew open at that moment. The housekeeper, dressed in a voluminous green robe, took one look at them standing by the crib and crossed the room in a half-dozen sturdy steps. "Give me the little lamb," she crooned. Brady looked at Lara, who nodded. Reluctantly, he handed the child over, amazed at how empty his hands and arms suddenly felt.

"I was downstairs in my room," Myra said, expertly wrapping Nathan in a blanket. "I heard breaking glass.

When I went to look, I found the window in the sitting room with a hole—"

Brady left without hearing the rest, taking the stairs two at a time. Armstrong had known Lara was back in town—did he also know about Nathan? He'd talked about an eye for an eye...

"The sitting room is to the right," Lara said. She'd followed him down the stairs. There was no color in her face and her eyes were wide. He moved into the formal Victorian sitting room lit only by a glass-shaded table lamp. Shards of glass lay on the table and carpet and a rock with a paper tied around it had tumbled to a stop on the floor in front of the table.

Myra, still holding Nathan, arrived in the doorway as Lara leaned down to pick up the rock. Brady grabbed her hand. He looked around the room until he spied a small lace doily draped over the armrest of a floral love seat. Using a corner of the doily, he picked up the rock and slipped the paper from beneath the rubber band.

"What does it say?" Lara asked, her voice little more than a whisper.

He angled the paper toward the light. A few words had been cut from a magazine and glued in place. "'Go home before it's too late,'" he read.

"Mrs. Kirk will have a fit when she hears someone broke her window," Myra fumed. She held Nathan against her polyester-covered bosom as though protecting him from the hounds of hell. "What is the world coming to? And that note can't be directed at Lara. It must mean you, Mr. Skye. What trouble have you brought—"

"Get a paper bag big enough for the rock and the note, will you please?" Brady interrupted.

Myra looked from him to Lara. "That's a good idea,"

Lara said, holding out her good arm. Myra very gently placed Nathan in Lara's embrace before leaving the room. Lara's eyes glistened in the dim light as she rested her cheek atop Nathan's fuzzy head.

Brady looked down at his shoes, not trusting his voice. What a sight the two of them made. His wife and his baby son. Her beauty, his innocence, elicited a cavalcade of emotions.

How had things gotten to this point? How had he so thoroughly screwed up?

How had he lost them?

He finally managed to say, "Someone wants you to leave Riverport," and looked at Lara again. She'd closed her eyes as though she couldn't stand to face another moment of this interminable night. She surprised him as she often did. Opening her eyes and pinning him with her gaze, she said, "That's too bad. I'm not going anywhere until I'm damn good and ready."

"Listen to me, Lara. This isn't just about you and me anymore, it's about Nathan now, too. Let me stay the night. Let me—"

"Okay."

"No argument?" he asked, surprised she was agreeing so readily.

"No argument. I'm not a complete idiot. But who would do something like this?" She moved a few inches closer to him and he took comfort that she still found his presence reassuring. "You said Bill Armstrong would try to get back at you. Do you think it was him?"

"I don't know," he hedged. Of course he thought it was Armstrong. But the thought of giving Lara more ammunition to feed the fear behind her eyes just seemed cruel to him.

"Are you going to give the rock and the note to the police?"

"You should give them to the police and report this incident, but I doubt anything will come of it. Maybe Tom could talk to Armstrong, that might help."

"Maybe I could talk to Mr. Armstrong."

Brady looked from Nathan's yawn to Lara's eyes. "No. Absolutely not. The man isn't thinking clearly. Please, stay away from him." He touched Nathan's tiny fist. "Think of this little guy."

She instantly bristled. "I seldom think of anyone else," she said.

He counted to ten under his breath, biting back the words that would just drive them further apart. But whose fault was it she felt alone in parenthood? Sure as hell wasn't his, he hadn't had a choice.

Sure you did. You sent her away.

She yawned, which destroyed the haughty look she'd affected. His defenses immediately fell. "Maybe you should try to get some sleep."

She nodded as she gathered the baby closer. He fought off the desire to wrap his arms around them both. What would he give for an invitation to join her in her bed?

A right arm? A left leg? How about a heart?

"Good night, Brady."

"Good night."

She left as Myra entered, pausing just a second to ask Myra to get Brady a pillow and blanket and anything else he needed for the night. To Brady, it appeared Myra vacillated between delight that he wasn't going back to Lara's room and distress he would still be under the same roof.

Myra crossed the room and handed him the paper bag. He dropped in the rock and the note.

"What do you need for tonight?" Myra snapped. Her constant antagonism was beginning to wear a little thin.

"Not a thing," he told her, relieved when she bustled off, muttering to herself under her breath.

LARA HAD THOUGHT she'd have a terrible time getting to sleep. She'd assumed unconsciousness would bring back those few moments in the submerged car. Plus, the burning pain in her arm made finding a good position to rest almost impossible.

But fall asleep she did and so deeply that she didn't wake until the first light filtered through the bedroom window. As Nathan usually provided the morning get-out-of-bed alarm, she immediately got up and crossed the room to the crib, holding her injured arm against her side. The throbbing started the moment she stood.

"Hey, sleepyhead," she crooned as she approached, her blue nightgown silky against her legs.

The crib was empty. She turned so abruptly she almost tripped on her own feet. Within a few seconds, she'd sprinted through her bedroom door and halfway down the stairs. "Myra," she called, growing more and more frantic at the still, watchful feeling of the house. A million what-ifs? darted through her head.

Myra appeared from the direction of the kitchen, a dishrag in her hand, a finger against her lips. Lara caught herself on the last step. Myra nodded toward the study on the opposite side of the foyer from the sitting room.

Brady sat in the one man-size chair her mother had in the house. Nathan lay against his chest, his father's big hands clutched around his tummy, his head tipped over to one side, like Brady's. They were both sound asleep.

With a jolt that shook her deep inside, Lara stared at the two of them. This was what had been missing for the past three months: the two of them together.

Her husband, Nathan's father. This was the picture that hadn't been taken and tacked in the baby book, the image she'd never dared to contemplate.

"They were down here when I got up this morning," Myra said. "I left well enough alone. I hope that's okay."

"Of course it's okay," Lara said, her heartbeat erratic as she fought a groundswell of inappropriate feelings. Father and son…

"You can't trust him," Myra said very softly. "He's just like his father—"

"No," Lara said succinctly. "No, Myra, he is not just like his father. And more importantly, he is Nathan's daddy. Brady and I aren't together anymore, but that doesn't mean you can be rude to him. If that's too much to ask of you, I'll go to a motel."

"Now, Miss—"

Lara rubbed her forehead. The beginnings of a headache pulsed behind her eyes. "I'm sorry. I shouldn't snap at you. This is more your house than it is mine."

"If he's good enough for you, well, then…" Myra's voice faded as though she couldn't bear to complete the phrase. She cast a raised eyebrow at Lara's scanty nightgown and added, "If you want to get dressed, I'll start breakfast."

"Thanks," Lara said.

She went back upstairs and dressed. Myra appeared

after a few minutes, Nathan in her arms, her face set in yet another frown. "That man took over the cooking," she said.

"He has a way with fried potatoes," Lara said as she started diapering Nathan.

Myra shooed her away. "I'll take care of the angel, you take care of the devil in the kitchen," she snapped.

Lara couldn't help but laugh.

Brady knew exactly how she liked the potatoes, crispy and redolent with onion. He executed their preparation perfectly. They sat across the informal kitchen table from each other without saying much. The trouble wasn't a lack of conversational material, Lara reflected as she buttered her toast. The trouble was there was too much that needed to be said.

The domesticity of sharing a meal, especially breakfast, at a small table in a room filled with homey smells, was daunting. It reminded Lara of other days, of other dreams. A half-dozen times she opened her mouth and closed it without speaking. She owed him an explanation, she knew that, but where to start, how to justify her actions? They'd made sense at the time. Now she wasn't so sure.

"I called the hospital," Brady said.

She looked up. "How's Jason?"

He laid down his fork and picked up the coffee mug. "He's still alive but unconscious. The police have stationed a guard at the boy's door. They want you to come by this morning, to the station, I mean. You need to give them a statement about last night. So do I."

"Okay. It's good about the guard, though, right?"

"It'll keep whoever shot him from finishing the job." He took a swallow of Myra's hair-on-your-chest brew and added, "You might as well know I don't intend to sit around waiting for something else to happen."

"Good. What's step one?"

"Ask questions. Ruffle feathers, starting with Bill Armstrong."

"Is it smart for you to talk to him yourself?"

"Probably not. I don't want to egg him on. I'll get Tom to have a chat with him. And then I intend to question Jason's old girlfriend. Maybe he told her whatever it was he was going to tell you last night. If Armstrong is losing control, the sooner he's stopped, the better."

"I still don't know what he hoped to gain by throwing that rock and making idle threats."

"Maybe they weren't idle threats. Anyway, even though the note had to be thought out ahead of time because of the way it was constructed, I don't think Armstrong really has a plan, I think he's just reacting to everything as it happens." He put the cup down and added, "Do you know this Wylie girl?"

"From the teen center, you mean? I think so. I think she hung out with Jason's sister. There was a small group of girls from the same neighborhood who used to come in together."

Myra stepped into the kitchen. "The little darling went back to sleep," she said. "I swear, Miss Lara, that baby is perfect."

"Even though he's a Skye?" Brady asked with a little of the old glint in his dark eyes.

Lara shot him a warning look.

"As far as I'm concerned, he's a Kirk," Myra said, banging a few pots in the sink.

Attempting to defuse a potential bomb, Lara addressed the surly housekeeper. She'd known the woman wouldn't be able to keep her antagonism at bay. "Do you know the Wylie girl's first name?"

"The older one or the younger one?"

"The one who's sixteen or seventeen?"

"Seventeen. Her name is Karen. The older one is married and lives in Portland. The mother takes in sewing at her house."

"I'm going to drop the note off with Tom and then go talk to Karen Wylie," Brady said, pushing his plate away. "It's summer vacation, maybe she's helping her mother."

"If Myra will watch Nathan for a little while, I'll go with you," Lara said. Maybe alone in a car, Brady and she could begin the delicate business of coming to grips with shared parenthood.

"The girl might feel more comfortable talking to you," Brady said. "But I have to go by work first and make sure everyone is on target."

"Good thing we're getting an early start."

Myra, scraping plates into the sink, looked over her shoulder. "After Nathan's nap, I'll put him in that fancy stroller you brought and we'll go next door to meet my friend, Barb. That would be okay, wouldn't it, Miss Lara?"

Lara could see that Brady was about to come up with a reason that wouldn't be okay, so she quickly jumped in with an answer. "That would be fine."

Brady glowered.

THEY ARRIVED at the Good Neighbors house at the same time as the supply truck filled with used brick. Brady spent a few minutes signing papers and double-checking job assignments before informing his foreman he'd be back later.

The drive out to Tom's place was full of starts and stops conversation wise. Brady could tell Lara was trying to find a way to talk to him about Nathan. He couldn't think of one thing she had to say that he wanted to hear, at least not about how she'd hidden her pregnancy and his baby from him. Not right now.

He'd lingered outside Lara's room most of the night, sitting in an uncomfortable chair so he wouldn't fall asleep. When he'd heard the baby fussing, he'd tiptoed into the room and plucked him from the crib, carrying him down the stairs, anxious for just a few moments alone with the little guy before he was forced to wake Lara to take care of needs Brady wasn't sure how to fill.

But Nathan hadn't kept fussing, he'd calmed right down and been wide awake. There in the study, his knees drawn up to make a lap, Brady had spent the better part of an hour interacting with his son. Eventually, they'd both fallen asleep in the chair. Brady hadn't woken until Lara's voice invaded his dreams.

He'd heard her defending him to the housekeeper. He'd kept his eyes closed, but her words had been comforting. She'd defended him and he didn't want her ruining it now by trotting out a bunch of lame excuses. So he switched on the radio and kept his eyes on the road and eventually she gave up trying to be heard over the country-western station. Fine with him.

Tom lived in a small house at the end of a long driveway. The house, painted white twenty years earlier, was dingy now. There was no garage but there was a large shop that Kenny used to work on cars.

The new red SUV was parked in front of the house. Lara stayed in the truck as Brady knocked on the door. Tom didn't answer, which didn't surprise Brady. He knew from his own shift work that Tom had worked most of the night and would probably sleep away most of the morning.

Brady made a cursory check of the shop just to make sure Tom wasn't out pulling an all-nighter on one of his projects. He saw a dark sedan with the engine hood open and a small car under a tarp, but no Tom. He was halfway back to the truck when the house door opened a crack and Tom looked out.

Brady veered toward the house. Tom, opening the door a few inches, called, "Thought I heard someone pounding on my door."

"Sorry about that," Brady said.

"You been out at the shop?"

"Yeah. Looks like you've got several projects going on out there."

"I like to keep busy."

"What's under the tarp?"

"I'm putting in a new clutch for Caroline," he said, rolling his eyes, his usual reaction when referring to his ex-wife. "Her warranty just ran out. The damn woman drives like a maniac. What brings you out here?"

Brady told him about the night before and his suspicions about who was behind the incident.

"Damn fool," Tom said around a yawn.

"I was going to talk to him—"

Tom shook his head. "Absolutely not. Stay away from Bill Armstrong."

"That's why I'm here," Brady said, jaw clenched. "To ask you to talk to him." His temper was right at the edge, and whether it was there because of lack of sleep or Tom's attitude or tension over Lara, he didn't know.

"Just you stay away from him. After following the

Briggs kid last night, all you need to do is to get in Bill Armstrong's face today. Dixon would love that. Leave it to me. Get Lara to take the rock and note to the station and report the incident so it's on record just in case. And Dixon is expecting you to come in and talk to him."

"I know."

They drove back into town in more silence. Brady made a quick stop to get the glass to fix Lara's mother's window, then parked at the station. They separated at the door. Brady cooled his heels for thirty minutes before Dixon had time to talk to him.

In his fifties, Chief Dixon was as tall as Brady but twenty-five pounds lighter. He sported a beak nose, dangerous little black eyes, thin lips and teeth stained by tobacco.

"Sit down, Skye," Dixon said, using his smoldering cigarette to point at the empty chair across his desk.

Brady leaned against the wall. "This is fine."

Dixon got to his feet, thumbed open a file on his desk, scanned the pages and closed the file. "What were you doing following Jason Briggs?"

Brady repeated his story in as much detail as possible. He knew Dixon had already read the reports and nothing he said was new. The fact he'd spent so many hours less than a year ago standing in this office having similar conversations with Dixon about Billy Armstrong just made the situation all the more uncomfortable.

Dixon led him through his story another time or two. "You're sure you weren't jealous?" Dixon finally said.

"Of what?"

"Of this kid spilling his guts to Lara Kirk instead of you."

"Jealous enough to shoot him and leave her and him both to drown?"

Dixon puffed on his cigarette and didn't blink.

Brady finally said, "No. I wasn't jealous. And I don't carry a gun around, you know that."

Dixon stubbed his cigarette out with Smokey the Bear thoroughness. "Yesterday you told Tom James to watch out for the Kirk woman and the Briggs boy. That was smart. But last night you got creative and put yourself on the scene of an attempted murder. That was dumb, even for you."

Brady pushed himself away from the wall. "If I hadn't 'gotten creative' as you say, you'd have a double homicide on your hands. Two dead bodies instead of two wounded ones. You do know that, right?"

Dixon sprang to his feet and leaned over his desk. "The Riverport Police Department doesn't need help from people like you, *Mr.* Skye."

"People like me," Brady mused. "Oh, you mean people who rescue other people from certain death?"

"What I mean is civilians. Stay away from everyone involved in this case, because it seems a little peculiar you were on hand on two separate occasions when two kids took a bullet. Any more little coincidences and I'll have you sitting in my jail. It wouldn't be the first time I entertained a Skye."

What could you say to that? "What about Bill Armstrong? Has anyone asked him where he was last night?"

"That's none of your business."

Knowing there was nothing to be learned from Dixon, Brady left the office. He was annoyed with himself for letting Dixon goad him into bragging. When he'd first become aware Dixon didn't like him, he'd tried to figure out why. Talk about hitting your head against a brick wall. All he knew was his father and Dixon had a history of sorts and loathed one another.

Apparently, Dixon had taken that hatred and passed it along to his nemesis's sons. There was no way to fight an unreasonable hatred like that, especially when it was your boss. You learned to live with it. After Brady quit, he'd heard tales Dixon took the department out to celebrate.

Lara waited in the lobby and just looking at her did a lot to calm the raging-lava flow in his gut. She carried a plastic bag through which he could see her soggy handbag and one ruined sandal.

"How was Dixon?" she asked once they were back inside the truck.

"Charming as always. Warned me to stay away from everyone connected to the case."

"Will you?"

He flashed her a smile. "Hell, no."

"He hates you."

"And my father."

She touched his arm after checking a few numbers jotted on a paper. "That must be the Wylie house. The yellow one."

Brady pulled up in front of a tiny square tract house. A narrow driveway and a converted garage ran along the east side. A sign over the door of the garage read, Lucinda's Alterations and Original Designs. Another sign announced the place was open for business.

The converted work space was small and cluttered with bolts of fabric, piles of clothing and other sewing paraphernalia. A large worktable held an industrial-looking sewing machine, behind which sat a woman, facing the door. She looked up as they entered, smiled warmly, finished sewing something, snapped the threads and stood. In her mid-forties, her face was thin, her eyes a grayish-blue. Blond hair streaked with silver fell in loose waves.

She stepped out from behind the machine. "Can I help you?"

"Mrs. Wylie?"

"Call me Lucinda," she said. "Everyone does."

Brady introduced Lara and then himself. By now, he knew he should be used to the way people looked twice when he gave his name. Face it, in this town his name would always be linked with Billy Armstrong's death.

But the truth was, he wasn't used to it and Lucinda Wylie's renewed spark of interest as she apparently figured out where she'd heard his name before made him squirm inside his skin. Staying in Riverport was a constant lesson in humility.

"If it's okay with you, we'd like to talk to Karen," Lara said.

Lucinda Wylie's eyes narrowed. "Why?"

"I used to work at the teen center," Lara said. "I knew Sara Armstrong and your daughter and a couple of the other girls."

Lucinda produced a tissue from her apron pocket and dabbed at her eyes. "That was so tragic about Sara. She was such a sweetheart. And her folks. Her mother is a saint, poor woman, and Bill Armstrong is all bluster on the outside and such a sweetheart underneath. The kids all love that man. He used to be like a father to Karen and my older daughter, Joanie. My husband's been gone ten years and, well, Bill was just wonderful with them. To lose Sara like he and Sandra did and then Billy—"

Too late she seemed to realize she was talking in front of the man who had killed Billy. Her gaze shifted uncomfortably in Brady's direction, then down to her feet.

Brady did his best not to look as confused as he felt. In his head, Armstrong didn't fit the teddy-bear image Lucinda described.

"I talked to Jason Briggs for a few minutes last night," Lara said.

Lucinda's brow wrinkled. "Then he's out of detention?"

"Just barely. He had something he wanted to tell me. He mentioned your daughter's name."

Lucinda shook her head. "Karen broke up with Jason while he was in juvie. Frankly, I was glad she did. I thought he was a bad influence on her. Now, I don't know."

"Before he could tell Lara what he wanted, someone took a shot at him," Brady said.

Lucinda gasped. "I didn't know that. Is he okay?"

"He's in the hospital."

Lucinda seemed to shrink. "You don't think Karen had anything to do with—"

"No, of course not," Lara assured her. "I was just hoping Jason might have told Karen why he wanted to see me. Is it okay with you if Brady and I talk to her for a few moments? You're welcome to be present—"

A sharp bark of humorless laughter escaped Lucinda's lips. Her hand flew to cover her mouth. "Okay with me? Karen does what she wants when she wants. She has a job down at the pharmacy. She'll talk to you if she feels like it. Otherwise, wild horses won't be able to drag a word out of her."

"Has she always been—"

"Difficult? Touchy? Secretive?" Lucinda interrupted. "Not always. After Jason got in trouble she kind of changed. After he went to juvie. She hasn't seen him since he got out."

"Are you sure?" Brady asked.

Lucinda's smile was bittersweet. "The only thing I'm sure of is that Karen's headed for trouble if she doesn't straighten herself out. Go ahead, try talking to her. She takes a lunch break about eleven-thirty."

Chapter Five

While Lara fed the baby, Brady fixed the window in the sitting room. He could hear Lara singing to Nathan. The song was a little nursery tune he vaguely recalled and he wondered if his mother had ever sung it to him.

She was gone now, so he'd never know. But even if she hadn't died, it would be a lost cause to ask her. His childhood memories had been soaked up by gin two dozen years before.

If this was the kind of baggage a little song dug up, Brady reflected as he tapped the glass into place, no wonder Lara had hidden her pregnancy from him.

Within an hour, they were both ready to catch Karen Wylie before her break. This time Lara chatted nonstop during the drive, flicking off the radio when he turned it on. To his relief, she seemed more interested in talking about Lucinda Wylie than their current mess.

"That poor woman is in over her head," Lara said as Brady parallel parked a few doors down from the drugstore. He immediately spied Tom's red SUV parked a few spots down and next to it, Bill Armstrong's black truck.

"She's lost control of her kid, that's for sure," Brady

said. What he wanted to do was march down the block and confront Bill Armstrong. His feet fairly itched with the desire to take him that direction. It went against every grain in his body to leave his problems to someone else to fix, even Tom. And doing what Dixon wanted always felt wrong.

But he didn't. His better sense had driven him to involve Tom and he would behave himself. The situation was just so damn frustrating.

"What are you looking at?" Lara asked as her gaze followed his.

"That black truck belongs to Bill Armstrong. Tom is apparently meeting with him. I'm sorry, I lost the thread of what you were saying."

"I was feeling sorry for Lucinda Wylie. Her daughter appears to be running wild."

"Just like my brother did," Brady said, looking at Lara. The truth was, the sight of her was no more comforting than the sight of Armstrong's truck. He was as powerless to touch her as he was Armstrong. "The difference is my parents didn't care when Garrett went off the deep end," he added.

"But *you* did," Lara said softly.

"Someone had to bail him out of trouble."

"And so it was you."

"Who else was there?"

"Have you heard from Garrett since, well, in the last year?"

"Not a word. Which one of us should quiz Karen?"

Lara opened her door but looked back at him. "Let's play it by ear."

Karen, a shorter, rounder version of her mother, stood behind a counter ringing up greeting cards for a woman with two little boys clinging to her legs. As soon as the mother and children left, Brady and Lara approached her. Karen met his gaze and immediately looked around the store as though making sure the pharmacist wasn't watching.

"You recognize me, don't you?" Brady asked.

She nodded. She had a plump, pretty face with pink pouty lips and hair bleached to platinum with black roots.

"I'd like to ask you a few questions," Brady said.

The girl looked from him to Lara and back again. "You ain't a cop no more," she said while biting her chewed-off thumbnail. "I don't have to answer your questions."

"No, you don't. That's true. Did you know your boyfriend, Jason Briggs, was—"

She stopped gnawing on her nail. "Jason ain't my boyfriend. We broke up months ago."

"I'm sorry, I meant to say your ex-boyfriend," Brady said calmly.

She shrugged. She wore a tight pink camisole under her pharmacy coat and a heart suspended on a silver chain. Brady suspected Lucinda Wylie was right to worry about her youngest daughter.

"How about we treat you to lunch?" Lara said.

"I ain't going to lunch. I'm on a diet."

"We really do need to ask you a few questions about Jason. You know he's in the hospital, don't you?"

Her heavily made-up eyes widened. "What happened to him? I saw him riding his bike yesterday. He looked okay."

"Someone shot him last night," Brady said.

The girl's knuckles turned white as she gripped the counter harder. "I didn't know. Is he going to be okay?"

"I hope so," Brady said. "But right now his condition is serious."

The front door opened to admit three people. One was a teenage boy who greeted Karen by name, the others were an older couple who made their way to the back of the store to the prescription counter.

"I gotta get back to work now," Karen said. "If Mr. Jones sees me standing around talking, he'll fire me. You guys should leave."

"It'll only take a second. Did Jason talk to you after he got out of detention?"

She shrugged. "Kind of. So what?"

Lara's voice was matter-of-fact as she said, "Did he mention he was going to see me last night?"

Karen shrugged again. "Maybe."

"Did he tell you why?"

The boy approached the counter, his gaze glued to Karen. She flashed him a million-watt smile and turned back to Lara. "I told you, I got to work now."

"How about we meet you after work?" Lara asked. "We'll buy you a cold drink next door. We'll only take five minutes of your time."

The teen put a pack of gum on the counter and pushed it toward Karen.

"Okay, whatever," Karen said, her eyes now on the boy.

"What time?" Brady asked.

"Three o'clock," she said. "I'll meet you next door."

"We'll be there," Lara said.

MYRA HAD ALREADY DONE the dishes, given the baby a bath and put on a load of laundry, so there wasn't much for Lara to do. Living this way was a far cry from her life up in Seattle where nothing got done unless she did it. It did lend insight as to why her mother traveled so much, however. With Myra taking care of the home front it was either travel or join clubs, and her mother wasn't one for community service.

With no chores to do, Lara called the hospital and got a very terse reply to her question about Jason's condition. "No change," is what the nurse on duty said. It was clear that was all she would say.

Lara spent the next hour on the phone with the towing and insurance companies. The car was less than a month old and was a complete write-off. Good thing she had a great policy. She was assured a rental would be delivered later that day, which she could use until she bought a replacement.

Money was never much of an issue for Lara seeing as she had inherited a sizable trust from her father when she turned twenty-one. Her mother had hinted the trust was the main reason Brady had wanted to marry her. Lara had always known that wasn't true. Men like Brady didn't live off their women.

Since Brady had taken off to check in on his construction project, Lara settled Nathan on a blanket under the tall trees in the side yard. It was so hot she stripped him down to his diaper and he reacted as he usually did to little or no clothes by kicking his legs. She leaned over him and talked nonsense, delighting in his drooly smiles as he grabbed fistfuls of her hair and squealed with delight.

She finally lay back on the blanket and closed her eyes. Her arm throbbed in time with her heartbeat.

How much longer should she stay in Riverport?

It had been less than twenty-four hours since she'd

shared news of Nathan's existence with Brady. How could she now even think of taking him three hours away? But how could she stay in Riverport and live this close to the daily temptation of Brady Skye?

She'd been worried he would misread her coming back to town as an attempt at reconciliation. That couldn't happen, she wouldn't allow it to happen. Feelings didn't matter at times, and one of those times was when trying to make a long-term decision that impacted an innocent child. Brady couldn't even hold a real conversation with her. His instinct to avoid confrontation had him turning up the radio and changing the subject every time she tried to broach their very real problems.

He thought he was protecting her, but it felt like isolation.

She understood where he was coming from. He'd grown up holding everyone in his family together by the sheer force of his will. He'd presented his family's public face to the world and even though it hadn't fooled anyone, he'd kept it up long after his family fell apart.

But her role now was tricky. Tricky to remain impassive when her heart leaped in her chest if he looked at her a certain way. Tricky to stand close to him without leaning, tricky to be near him, to share Nathan without entertaining foolish dreams.

She sat up abruptly and hugged her knees as she studied her drowsy son. She'd told herself she was enough for him, she would be his world, he would be hers. And now she admitted the fallacy of this conclusion. Nathan had a father. And Brady wasn't the kind of man to settle for infrequent visits.

Which, face it, was the real reason she'd put this off for so long. She'd been waiting until she felt strong enough to face Brady and not fold.

Brady, Brady, Brady. She was suddenly very annoyed with the direction her thoughts always seemed to drift.

Better she should keep her mind on the bullet last night. On the broken window and the threat. Better she should remember someone had tried to kill Jason and had left her and the boy to drown. Why? What could Jason possibly have to say to her that deserved this kind of reaction and from whom? There had to be a reason.

Was Brady right? Was the culprit Bill Armstrong? Again, why?

Jason had been safely kept in detention since the accident. He'd only been out for a day or two when he was shot. Had that been Bill Armstrong's first opportunity to get at the boy he blamed for his son's death?

But Bill didn't blame Jason. According to Brady, he blamed Brady. He wanted to get back at Brady. And Brady was spending time with Lara. He'd shown up at the house minutes after she arrived in town yesterday and his truck had been parked outside last night when the rock sailed through the window. Maybe the bullets had been intended for her and not Jason. Maybe Jason was just a hapless bystander.

Her gaze traveled from the small dock built out over the river, to the heavily shaded gardens to the nearby road. At that moment, a black truck passed, going so slowly it had three cars backed up behind it.

Bill Armstrong drove a black truck.

So did dozens of other Riverport citizens.

Nevertheless, a chill ran down Lara's spine. The yard no longer felt like a sanctuary. She carefully scooped up Nathan. Holding him close to her chest, she hurried back inside while the black truck and its stream of followers continued down the road.

THEY SLID into a booth at exactly five minutes before three. At ten minutes after the hour, they faced the fact that Karen Wylie wasn't coming.

"Why would she skip out on us?" Lara asked, pushing away her untouched ice tea. They'd been discussing all the things Lara had thought about out in the yard—well, most of the things. She'd left out the personal stuff.

And she'd left out being spooked by a black truck. That was just too embarrassing to admit.

Brady drained his glass and put a five on the table. "Let's go find out."

They walked next door to find an older woman standing at the counter. While Brady looked around the pharmacy, Lara waited in line. The woman was a contemporary of Lara's mother, a woman in her fifties with bright red hair. She claimed she didn't have the slightest idea where Karen went, just that she'd been called in on her day off.

Brady was in the back, talking to the pharmacist. Hayden Jones had been filling prescriptions since before Lara was born. She started to make her way back as Brady shook Hayden's hand and met her midway. Taking her elbow, he guided her out onto the sidewalk. "Karen quit," he said, leaning down to talk close to her ear. He must have felt her startled response, for he pulled her against the building so pedestrians could pass them by.

Her response had been twofold. The news Karen was gone and the proximity of Brady's lips to her ear.

"She quit? Did Mr. Jones say why?"

"No. He said he saw her talking to us earlier today. After we left, she used the phone and then ten minutes later she told him she was quitting and proved it by walking out the door."

"Yet when we were there, she was worried talking to us might get her fired."

"Let's go talk to her mother."

This time the silence in the truck was fraught with an underlying tension that had nothing to do with their personal situation. For the second time that day, they entered the converted garage. As before, Lucinda Wylie looked up from her sewing machine. This time her smile of welcome faded a little when she saw who it was.

"She won't talk to you, huh? Well, don't look at me. I already told you I can't get her to do a damn thing she doesn't want to do."

"Is she here?" Lara asked. "Is she inside the house?"

"She's at work," Lucinda said, eyes narrowing. "Didn't you go there to talk to her?"

"She was kind of evasive. She finally agreed to meet us after work at three o'clock."

"That's news to me," Lucinda said as her gaze darted to the wall clock. It was almost four.

"She didn't show up," Brady said. "Hayden Jones said she left work before noon. In fact, she quit."

Lucinda immediately stood up, irritation erasing her weariness. "She quit? I can't believe she'd quit after everything I went through to get her hired on down there." She marched determinedly out from behind the sewing machine and across the room, opening the door with a vengeance. She crossed the driveway and climbed the two stairs to the backdoor of her small house, disappearing inside without a backward glance at Lara or Brady. The screen door slammed in her wake.

"She's not here," Lucinda said a moment later as she stared through the screen.

Brady crossed the driveway. "Can you tell if she came home after she left work?" he asked.

"Come in while I look," Lucinda said.

They stood in the neat, tiny kitchen while Lucinda opened a closet door and then went down a short hall. She reappeared in a moment. "She's been home. Her smock is on her floor as usual."

"Anything missing?" Brady asked. "A suitcase, clothes, money?"

"She doesn't have any money," Lucinda said, but as she spoke, she crossed to the closet and opened it again, this time taking out her handbag. She opened her wallet and groaned. "She took the hundred dollars I had in here for groceries."

"Look for her suitcase," Brady urged.

Muttering under her breath, Lucinda disappeared down the hall again. She came back a few minutes later empty handed. "The suitcase is gone. So are some of her clothes. Where did she go?"

"There was a boy in the pharmacy she seemed to know," Lara said. "About her age, tall and kind of skinny."

"You just described half the boys in this town," Lucinda said.

"Did she leave a note?" Brady asked.

Lucinda checked the chalkboard by the refrigerator. "This is where we always leave notes to one another. There's nothing here."

"Call her friends," Brady urged. "If you can't track her down, call the police. She's underage, get them to keep an eye out for her. I'll drive around and see what I can find."

"What did you two say to her?" Lucinda demanded.

"Just what we talked about with you," Lara said. "She was working and she didn't want to talk."

"But she ran away right after you spoke with her, isn't that what you said?"

"After she made a phone call," Brady answered.

Lucinda narrowed her eyes. "She hasn't been the same since Billy Armstrong was killed and Jason went away." This time, she uttered the comments without flinching, meeting Brady's gaze head-on as though challenging him to contradict her. Brady said nothing. Lara had to bite her lip to keep from leaping to his defense.

"Start calling around," Brady said. "I'll leave you my cell number."

THOUGH LARA HAD WANTED to come with him, Brady had convinced her that her place was at her mother's house with Nathan. He knew she was worried about Karen and what role their questions had played in her decision to bolt. Hell, so was he.

For a second, he just sat and stared at nothing. What was happening? How much danger was Lara really in? And Nathan? Wasn't any danger too much?

He wondered how Tom's talk with Armstrong had gone. Had Armstrong admitted anything, like cutting little words out of magazines and gluing them to paper?

Though it was almost an hour before the start of his shift, Tom's SUV was parked at the station. No way was

Brady going to risk running into Chief Dixon or anyone else for that matter. He'd talk to Tom later.

For an hour, he drove up and down every street in Riverport, looking for a bleached-blond teenager carrying a suitcase. Eventually, drenched with sweat and out of sorts, he pulled to the curb and stared at the street.

Why had Karen Wylie taken her mother's money and run out without even leaving a note? A suitcase implied an extended absence. Maybe she was taking a trip. The only way out of Riverport, besides private transportation, was by bus. Could she have taken the afternoon bus out of town?

Brady drove to the station, a narrow building sandwiched between other narrow buildings. The place only opened up when a bus arrived or departed. Brady lucked out. A bus had just pulled up outside and two or three passengers were disembarking, their wilted expressions reflecting the change from the air-conditioning inside the bus to the hundred-degree sidewalk temperature outside.

He went through the glass door into a room furnished in old plastic chairs and little else. A man who looked a decade beyond retirement age glanced up from his seat behind the grille at the ticket counter. Marking his place in a paperback book with a gnarled finger, he said, "Next bus to the coast leaves in ten minutes."

"When did the last bus leave?"

"That would be the twelve-fifteen, going the other direction to Portland. Say, aren't you that cop who was in the paper last year? Brady something. Skye. Brady Skye. I knew your granddad."

Brady trotted out one of his leftover police-issue smiles. His grandfather had been an upstanding member of the community, or so the community had thought. In truth, he'd been a gambler. Addiction ran heavy in the Skye family. It was why Brady never bought himself a beer or a lottery ticket. He hoped Garrett had the brains to do the same.

"I'm wondering if a girl purchased a ticket. Using cash, probably. Seventeen, bleached hair—"

"Looked twenty-five?" the old man interrupted.

Brady nodded.

"She sure did."

"Was she alone?"

"She was the one and only passenger, period," he said.

"Was the bus full?"

The old man shrugged. "Couldn't say. I never went out and looked. No one got off in Riverport."

"Did she buy a ticket all the way to Portland?"

"Yeah. 'Course, the bus stops at St. George and Scottsdell first."

Brady looked at the posted time schedule and then the wall clock. The bus had disgorged its Portland passengers a half hour before.

His thoughts were all over the place as he left the station. Now came the unpleasant task of telling Lucinda Wylie her daughter had left Riverport on a bus bound for Portland.

The question was, who was she running from? Or who was she running to? And, just as important, did her running away have anything to do with Jason Briggs's shooting? In other words, did Karen have anything to do with Jason's shooting or did she know who did?

He looked up just in time to see Bill Armstrong's black truck turn the near corner.

Chapter Six

"You scared her off somehow," Lucinda Wylie said for the fourth time, each repetition louder and more strident than the one before. "You find her."

Once again, Lara looked up and down the lazy evening street as she said, "Lucinda, come inside my mother's house and let me make you a cup of tea or pour you a glass of wine. Something. I don't know when Brady will be back. I don't like standing out here."

And she didn't. But Lucinda didn't even seem to hear her, she was too caught up in her own angst. Lara couldn't shake the feeling someone was watching. She'd been feeling that way all afternoon, ever since she allowed herself to get spooked by the black truck that had passed the house slowly. Even after she reminded herself Mr. Crowley lived a few doors down and always drove his black truck as though he was leading a funeral procession, the feeling had lingered.

Anxiety had nothing to do with rationale.

She repeated, "Please, come inside to wait."

"No, thank you," Lucinda said crisply. "The police

said they don't know if Karen got off the bus in Portland or somewhere before that. They said she left of her own free will and it's not a crime."

She'd said all this before, too. Lara fought the desire to yank the woman into the foyer or slam the door in her face. Instead, she tried to remember some of her counseling training. This woman needed help.

Before she could decide what to do next, Lucinda was off and running again. "The driver made a head count after each stop, but he has a schedule to keep, they said, so he would just keep going even if not everyone who was supposed to get on the bus didn't get on. If he did make note of someone not getting back on the bus, it would go to the bus line's head office in Arizona somewhere and it could take days—"

Lara grabbed Lucinda's hand. The woman was on the verge of hysteria. Lara said, "The police know Karen left. Eventually they'll look for her. Come inside and wait for Brady."

Both women turned as Brady's green truck rolled to a stop behind the new rental the leasing company had delivered an hour before. Thank heavens, Lara thought, sighing with relief. Even Lucinda looked hopeful.

It was seven o'clock, the night was warm and sticky, and as Brady walked across the lawn, he looked preoccupied. Lara felt a jab behind her ribs. The simple fact was her pleasure at seeing him surpassed just wanting him to deal with Lucinda Wylie.

He perked up a little when he met Lara's gaze and she chided herself. No matter how she struggled to keep her emotions to herself, she knew there were times he sensed exactly how she felt. It had always been like that between them and until a day ago, it hadn't mattered, at least not to her. She'd never kept secrets from Brady.

Okay, not true. She'd kept a whopper, but not while living in the same town with him.

"Have you heard from Karen?" he asked, turning his attention to Lucinda as he jogged the last few feet.

Lucinda, lips compressed into a straight line, said, "I'll tell you what I told her. You two scared my kid into leaving town, you find her and bring her back."

To Lara's amazement, Brady said, "I'll try."

Lara opened her mouth to protest, but one look at Brady convinced her otherwise. Who was she to ask him not to go? He felt responsible for the teen's abrupt departure from Riverport. So did she.

Lucinda said, "Oh, thank you, thank you. I was going to ask Bill Armstrong to go but he's not home. I don't know who else to ask." She began repeating what the police had told her and Brady listened as though he didn't know their procedures by heart.

"I'll go to St. George and Scottsdell and look around," Brady said. "Once the police figure out Karen was Jason Briggs's old girlfriend, I have a feeling their interest in her whereabouts will pick up and they'll try harder to find her. Until then, I'll do what I can, but I'm not promising anything."

Lucinda visually bit back tears. "I know she didn't hurt anyone."

Brady walked Lucinda to her car and came back to Lara shaking his head. She took his hand and pulled him inside the quiet house. Nathan was asleep, Myra was on watch. She sighed as the door shut behind them, glad to get behind a closed door.

"Where have you been?" she asked.

A smile chased away a little of his fatigue. "Were you worried about me?"

It was on the tip of her tongue to deny it, but she nodded instead.

"What's wrong?" he said, narrowing his eyes. "Something has you spooked. Was it Lucinda?"

"She's been out there threatening things for the past half hour."

"She's worried—"

"I know. I'm worried, too. Plus, there's this feeling I have. I don't know." Her voice trailed off.

He said, "What feeling? What aren't you telling me?"

"It's nothing. Just a feeling that someone is watching. Waiting."

"Did you see anyone?"

"Not really. I told you, it's just a feeling." She touched her bandaged arm. "I got spooked, is all."

"Maybe I shouldn't leave tonight."

"No, you should go. We have to try to help Lucinda and Karen. The thought of that kid out there alone makes me sick. She thinks she's so grown up."

"I know."

Anxious to get things back on an even keel before he left, she said, "What did you do this afternoon?"

"I asked around. Found out about the bus, told the cops. The police have asked the St. George, Scottsdell and Portland cops to keep an eye out for Karen, but it's a long shot. It's anyone's guess at this point if she got off the bus between here and the city and drove off with someone she went to meet, or went all the way to Portland and disappeared into the crowds there."

"Maybe she was going to meet someone who lives in St. George or Scottsdell."

"Maybe, but that means she wasted a lot of money on a ticket she didn't plan to use."

"Maybe the point was to throw her mother off."

"Maybe."

"Why are you going tonight? What do you hope to accomplish?"

"Frankly, I can't think what else to do." He stared at her a second before adding, "I'd like to have a few minutes with Nathan first. He and I kind of started getting to know one another during the night. Is it okay if I go find him?"

"You don't have to ask me if it's okay if you visit with your own son," she said.

"I wasn't sure."

They stood face-to-face in the cool foyer. She studied his face with an impersonal eye. Yesterday, after an absence of a year, he'd seemed a stranger to her. Today he was familiar again, the last year seemed to have passed in a haze.

He came a step closer, banishing the concept of semidetachment. "Last night I promised I wouldn't kiss you again," he whispered. "Now I wish I hadn't made that promise." His fingertips brushed her thighs as he touched her hands. Could he feel the little sparks that passed between them?

"I miss you, Lara, and damn it, you miss me, too, don't you?"

"That's not the point," she said.

"That's not the point? Our need for each other isn't the point?"

"No."

"You're going to have to explain that to me."

She didn't know how to explain it, not when it was

taking every ounce of willpower she had to stay on her feet and not melt into his arms.

The big clock right behind Lara ticked away the seconds. She forced herself to say, "Eventually, we have to have a real conversation about Nathan. We have to figure out how to share him."

"Share him without sharing each other, you mean."

"Don't make this harder than it already is, Brady."

He swallowed hard. "Okay. Your rules."

"I tried to tell you yesterday that I didn't come here to get back together. I came to correct the wrong I made. When you stop being so angry with me, we'll talk."

They both became aware of footsteps on the stairs and turned to find Myra descending, carrying Nathan. The baby's cheeks were flushed from sleep. His fist, crammed into his mouth, muffled the little whimpering sounds he made when he woke up hungry.

Brady said, "Hey, little man, what's wrong?"

At the sound of his father's voice, Nathan's grumblings disappeared.

Brady held out his hands and Nathan kicked his feet in anticipation.

Myra stepped off the stairs, glanced at Lara, and relented. Brady gently took the baby. Myra traveled on toward the kitchen, casting a surly frown over one shoulder.

Brady made a face at Nathan and the baby laughed.

"That's the first time he's ever done that," she said, kissing Nathan's bare foot.

"Laughed? Well, maybe some of his good taste will rub off on his momma." He snuggled Nathan, who gurgled again, a deep sound that for pure joy rivaled any sound Lara had ever heard. Brady was a natural.

She'd wondered, of course. She'd heard the horror stories of his youth, she knew how he'd struggled with two drunks as parents and a brother running out of control. But watching him now she decided there must have been some good years, too. Years when he and Garrett were babies and their parents weren't so dysfunctional.

Or was it all Brady, did it all come from his instincts, his heart, his love?

Clutching the baby firmly in his big hands, he held him a few inches over his own head and then lowered him close enough to kiss, and all the while he talked. He told the baby about his day, about the conversations he'd held with various people, about his plans for the evening, including Lara in the proceedings with occasional glances and comments about Mommy.

Brady had gone from lover to father in the beat of a heart. It was disconcerting.

And just the kind of thing Lara knew she had to steel herself against. It was no secret to her that she still found Brady Skye beguiling. That she still lusted after him and dreamed about him, and wished a hundred times a day he wanted a woman to share his life with, the good and the bad, and not packed away in tissue paper.

"Humor me and stay away from the windows tonight," Brady said as he finally handed back a cooing Nathan. As soon as Lara touched him, the baby started whimpering again, his hunger reawakened. She held him very close as though the sweet nearness of him could protect her from both his father's charms and his scary warnings.

Brady's eyes met hers as he added, "Don't wait up."

THE DRIVE WAS a fool's errand and was made as much to get away from the entanglements in his personal life as it was with any real hope he'd find Karen Wylie.

He drove slowly through both small towns and then on to Portland where he checked out the bus station and hoped to hell the kid was off the black streets.

· On the drive back to Riverport, he organized his thoughts into a string of events. Jason, out of detention, calls Lara. Lara comes back to town to speak with the boy. Someone shoots Jason and wings Lara. Armstrong makes threats, reveals he knows Lara's back in town. The rock, the threat. A very brief talk with Jason's ex-girlfriend. The girlfriend makes a call, steals money from her mother and bolts.

Why?

The most likely reason—Karen Wylie knew something about the shooting that made her nervous.

He thought again about her reaction upon learning Jason had been shot. Damn, he'd bet money her reaction had been genuine. She'd looked and acted stunned.

So, did someone think she knew something?

Or did she think she knew who was responsible and she was afraid of them?

There were too many variables. He wasn't sure.

It was two in the morning when he drove back into Riverport. There was really no reason to detour past the Kirk house as Tom had said they'd have someone drive by it every hour or so. He did anyway.

Lara had apparently pulled the rental car into her mother's garage. All the lights were off. Brady glanced down the side street and kept going. He circled the block and parked. He got out of his truck. He wore black jeans, a black T-shirt. He closed the door quietly and walked down the alley, eyes and ears adjusting, blending into the dark.

He wasn't sure why he was out here skulking around, just that there was no better way to find someone where they shouldn't be than by being there yourself. He stood in the cross street on a stretch of black pavement. There was no traffic. Nothing moved in the heavy air. No sounds, not even a dog or the nearby river.

As he watched, a light flicked on somewhere on the second floor. He took out his cell phone and dialed Lara.

She answered on the second ring. "Brady?"

"Yeah, it's me."

"Where are you?"

"Outside. No, don't draw back the curtain. Are you okay?"

"I'm fine."

"Is Nathan right there with you?"

"Yes. In fact, he's in bed with me. I think I have you to thank for his sudden desire for middle of the night tête-à-têtes."

"How about the housekeeper?"

"I heard her use the bathroom a little while ago. Brady, what's going on?"

Brady rubbed between his eyes. He stared at the house and the grounds for what seemed a week. Nothing moved. He finally said, "Give Nathan a kiss for me and try to get some sleep. I'll talk to you tomorrow."

"Brady?"

"It's okay. Honest." He clicked off the phone. As he slipped it into his pocket, he heard an engine rev. Bright lights shone all around him.

He turned to find a vehicle approaching with the speed of a tornado. He barely had time to jump to the side. The roar behind him convinced him to keep going. The vehicle jumped the curb. Brady kept running, not daring to look back, diving into the hedge in front of the neighbor's house. The headlights blinded him as the vehicle missed him and the bushes by inches. Brady pushed himself up off the ground. He'd fallen against a water spigot and banged his elbow. His right knee had apparently hit the edge of a brick as the denim was torn and bloody. He peered through the leaves in time to see two red taillights disappearing down the street.

He sat up, fighting to catch his breath. Lights flicked on in the house in whose hedge he squatted. After a few moments, the porch light came on and the door opened. Pajama bottoms and slippers shuffled into view. After a minute or two, the homeowner stepped back into the house, slammed the door and pushed the dead bolt home. Brady waited until the lights went off again before finally moving out of the hedge. Limping, he made his way across the street.

Lara opened the door before he could knock. He fell into her arms.

WAKING UP in Lara's bed wasn't the treat Brady knew it could be. Of course, the fact she wasn't in bed beside him might have something to do with that. She entered the room and sat down on the bed, flopping a paper bag on the floor.

"How do you feel this morning?"

Thinking of the way she'd so gently sponged off and bandaged his wounds the night before, the way her eyes had softened as she'd tucked him between her sheets, he said, "Hopeful."

"I thought you said you didn't find out a trace of Karen last night."

He stared at her a second and let it be. "I didn't. What's in the bag?"

"I used your keys to go to your place. You needed clean clothes," she said. "Then I went to the store and bought a new car seat for Nathan."

"You went out alone? After what happened to me in front of your house last night?"

"Yes. And I returned to tell the tale. Stop being so damn protective."

"How'd you know where I live?"

"I drove out to the house you're working on first and asked your foreman. He didn't know, so I called Tom and he told me."

"You didn't say anything about last night to Tom—"

"You asked me not to, so I didn't. I still think you should tell him."

"And explain why I was standing in the middle of the street in the middle of the night? No, thanks. I didn't see what kind of car or truck tried to run me down."

"Maybe there are tracks on the neighbor's lawn—"

"No," he repeated. "It could have been some plastered kid."

She narrowed her eyes. "You know it wasn't some kid."

"No, sweetheart, I don't know it wasn't some kid. Okay, it was probably Armstrong, but there's no way to know for sure."

"I give up. By the way, your foreman said he can handle things at the house today."

"Where's Nathan?"

"With Myra. If you get dressed quickly, I'll let you come with him and me to St. George and Scottsdell. I agree with you, there's no point trying Portland. It's too big. Let the police handle it."

He'd made the mistake of telling her he wanted to go back to the smaller towns at the same time of day the bus went through. It now appeared she'd commandeered the trip. He glanced at the bedside clock. Past eleven. He hadn't slept this late in years.

As Lara stood up, he threw back the covers. She didn't flinch despite the fact he wore nothing but his boxer shorts. Of course, it wasn't as though she hadn't seen him in a lot less than that.

"I think I should go alone," he said, pulling his jeans gingerly over the bandage covering his knee and getting to his feet to button them. Besides his knee, there were a few other scrapes on his legs and some blossoming bruises, but all in all, not as bad as he'd feared. "You and Nathan will be safer here—"

"Knock it off," she said, meeting his gaze straight on.

How could she resist him? That's what bugged him. Standing there so close one tiny nudge would have them touching, the energy between them so vibrant it burned away her flimsy dress. The memories so hot they sizzled.

She walked to the door and looked back over her shoulder. "You have fifteen minutes until breakfast is ready."

And then she was gone.

Chapter Seven

Thanks to the twisty river road, the bus never got up to speed. As Nathan dozed off in the back, secure in his brand-new baby seat, they discussed the right way to go about things. Lara finally admitted it made sense that one of them stay with Nathan and the car while the other scouted the area around each stop.

Brady's hope was that someone from the day before would be around today and that this someone might have noticed Karen Wylie. The police would talk to the bus driver when they located him, and eventually they'd do what Brady was doing, but Brady had a gut feeling time was of the essence.

The St. George stop was a coffee shop. After learning from the driver that he hadn't driven this route the day before, Brady followed the one departing passenger into the restaurant. The solitary waitress had been on duty the day before, but she didn't remember anyone getting off the bus. Brady talked to the busboy and even the cook, then he went outside as the bus pulled away from the curb.

He walked across the street and talked to the guy at the gas station, then into a small store where the clerk barely looked up from her magazine to answer a few questions. Outside again, he looked up and down the deserted street and couldn't think of anything else to do.

They caught up with the bus again five miles outside of St. George and followed it into Scottsdell where it stopped at a station even smaller than the one in Riverport. Nathan had woken up and was hungry, so while Lara nursed him, Brady got out of the car.

The driver had the baggage compartment open for the two passengers disembarking and the three catching the bus. Brady looked around to see who he might question. He'd start with the bead shop next to the station.

The woman in the bead store hadn't noticed the bus the day before for the simple fact she'd been closed. He tried a couple of other stores, back on the hot sidewalk a few minutes later. The bus was pulling away from the curb again and Brady was batting zero.

He spied a man standing on the far corner holding a sign. He approached, a few bills in his hand.

The sign said, "Out of gas, please help me get home to San Francisco."

"So, you're stranded here in Scottsdell, huh?" Brady said, stopping in front of the young man. He had longish brown hair and wore clothes the thrift shops would turn away. He smelled like old smoke, beer and culverts.

Looking at the money in Brady's hand, the man said, "I don't really have a car. But you're right, I am stuck."

Brady hadn't expected honesty. He handed over the money, which was pocketed with a mumbled thanks.

Brady finally said, "Were you standing out here yesterday?"

"And the day before that."

"Did you notice the bus come in?"

"You a cop?"

"Not anymore."

"Anyone in trouble?"

Brady shrugged. "Not really. A kid ran off and the mother is worried. That's all."

"A girl about nineteen or twenty?"

Brady's heart kicked up a few beats. "Close enough."

"Bleached hair."

"That's the one."

"I noticed her."

"Can you tell me what she did?"

The man narrowed his eyes. "She's in no trouble?"

"Not yet."

"She got off the bus carrying a little suitcase. I noticed it because she hadn't stowed it in the luggage compartment like the other lady who got off. The girl looked around, crossed the street and nodded at me."

"Did she say anything?"

"Nope. She waited on the next corner till the bus took off."

"And—"

"She stood there."

"For how long?"

"Don't know. Awhile. Then she started walking down toward the river."

"Did you watch her?"

"Yeah. There wasn't a lot else going on. I watched her until she got down near that warehouse."

Brady shaded his eyes. He could just see the dilapidated fence surrounding a large, low building. Vines baked to a brittle brown still clung to the fence.

"I looked away 'cause a car came up and a guy gave me a ten. By the time I looked back, the girl was gone."

"What do you mean, gone?"

"I couldn't see her anymore. I figured she caught a ride or something."

"And you didn't see her again."

"Nope. Listen, I don't want to get the kid in trouble. I say live and let live."

"And that's why I'm looking for her," Brady said.

As he walked back to the car, he wondered what had prompted him to spin the man's comment the way he had. Was he really afraid for Karen Wylie's life?

The answer was yes. In his years as a cop he'd learned to listen to his instincts and his instincts now were screaming at him to pin down this kid's location.

He looked up from these unsettling thoughts to find Lara had gotten out of the car with Nathan. She was perched against the hood, shaded by an old walnut tree. She held the baby close. He couldn't hear anything, but from the way her lips moved and her body swayed, he could tell she was singing to the baby.

The sight of the two of them caused a tiny fist to squeeze a drop of blood out of his heart.

"Karen got off the bus here and walked down near that warehouse," he told her, reaching for Nathan. She handed him the baby, who gurgled at Brady. "Let's walk down there and take a look," he added.

The three of them made their way five or six blocks down to the warehouse. Despite the heat and Brady's concern for Karen Wylie, that walk was one of the better walks Brady had ever taken. He loved the way Lara's stride matched his and he loved the soft weight of his son cradled in his arms. In a perfect world, they could have just kept walking, forever, maybe. That would have been fine with him.

They found a locked-up building plastered with several No Trespassing signs. Most of the windows appeared to be broken. The grounds were surrounded by a fence from which hung a very old-looking padlock.

Brady looked in a 360-degree circle, hoping to find someone else who might have seen Karen.

"How about that house across the street?" Lara said.

The Craftsman-style house looked as old as the warehouse. As they crossed the street, the door opened and an elderly woman wearing baggy hose and very large eyeglasses stepped onto her porch. "I saw you up there talking to that bum," she said by way of greeting. "He's been there all week. By now he could have bought a car with all the money suckers like you hand over."

Lara kind of froze in her tracks. Brady grinned. The woman was a snoop. Cops loved snoops. It made their jobs so much easier. He said, "I was asking him about a teenage girl who got off the bus yesterday about this time."

"That floozy. I saw her standing over there across the street until she walked off with that man."

"Did you see who she walked off with?" Brady said.

"Of course I did. Big man. Like you. Blue jacket with yellow doodads on it."

"Doodads?"

Her hands fluttered around the sleeves. "Doodads. Insignias maybe."

"Like military?"

"Maybe," she said, and for the first time, Brady noticed the thickness of her lenses and wondered how good her eyesight really was. "Did you recognize the man?"

"I never saw his face. He must have come up to her while I was looking away. By the time I saw them, they was walking the other direction."

"Could you tell how old he was?"

"He was wearing a cap and he never looked my way. He didn't walk like an old man. The two of them wandered off down that street over there."

"Is there anything else you can recall? A car—"

"A black truck?" Lara finished.

"My phone rang right then. That old fool Agnes was on the line. Claimed she caught her mailman peeking through her window. Last week it was the UPS man. Like they have nothing better to do than catch Agnes in her bloomers."

Brady thanked the woman and they walked back to the car, then drove down the street she had indicated. The houses quickly gave way to vacant lots.

"Dead end," Brady said.

"What now?"

"I'll tell Tom. Maybe he can talk to the Scottsdell sheriff."

"Won't Tom tell Dixon and won't Dixon come unglued you got in the middle of his investigation?" Lara asked as she looked over the seat to check on Nathan.

"Probably. Ask me if I care. They could have been here first if they thought it was important."

"I have a bad feeling about Karen Wylie," Lara said, settling back into the leather seat and frowning.

"I think she ran off with a new boyfriend," Brady said, glancing at Lara.

But the truth was, he had a bad feeling about the kid, too.

IT WAS WITH profound relief Lara watched Brady drive away to talk to Lucinda Wylie. When she'd learned Lara and Nathan would be gone all day, Myra had taken the day off and was even planning to spend the night with her sister. The house was all hers, Lara thought, hers and Nathan's.

She bathed her adorable son, laughed with him, fed him, then lay down beside him on her bed. After a few rousing games of patty-cake and a few kisses on his round tummy, Nathan's dark eyes—eyes like his father's minus about two hundred degrees of intensity—started to close.

As she silently watched slumber overtake him, she was stunned to feel tears burning behind her nose. No way was she going to lie there and blubber. Over what? What did she have to cry about? Karen's disappearance had been more or less explained. Brady, while still uncommunicative about their personal situation, was acting friendly enough. There was absolutely nothing to cry about.

How about the fact that you're losing a husband, that you are choosing to deny Nathan a chance to grow up in the same house with his father?

No. She'd already spent those tears. She pinched her nose and sat up, taking a few deep breaths in the bargain.

After she tucked Nathan into his crib, she washed her face, turned on the baby monitor, grabbed the handheld receiver and went downstairs.

What she needed was a project. Like sweeping a floor or starting dinner. Something normal with a beginning, middle and end.

As her foot hit the polished wood floor of the foyer,

a knock sounded on the front door and she opened it quickly, without thinking, not wanting the visitor to grow impatient and ring the doorbell and risk waking Nathan.

She didn't recognize the man at first. Hand on the doorknob, she stood facing him for the count of ten, taking in little about his appearance past his eyes and a scraggly sandy beard that ringed his gaunt face.

He said, "You're Lara Kirk."

She placed him at the sound of his voice. "Bill Armstrong," she said, recalling the day he'd come into the teen center, soon after his daughter died.

Just like Brady, Armstrong had changed in the past year, but in Armstrong, the change appeared to start and end in his eyes. Where before they'd burned with confusion and grief, they now seemed oddly flat.

"You remember me," he said.

"Of course I do." The big house loomed around her. The privacy she'd enjoyed a minute earlier now threatened to trap her. Hoping to hurry him along, she made her voice crisp. "What can I do for you, Mr. Armstrong?"

"I want to talk to Skye."

"He's not here," she said. "Try his house."

"He's not there. Everyone knows you two have taken up again. Everyone knows he's been living over here."

"That's not true," she said clearly. "But when I see him, I'll tell him you stopped by." She started to close the door. He caught the edge and met her gaze.

"What were you two doing in Scottsdell?"

She froze. "How—"

"I saw you," he said.

Once again she tried to close the door and once again he stopped her.

Annoyance tinged with alarm caused her to blurt out, "We talked to a woman in Scottsdell. She told us she saw a man about your size walking with a teenage girl who's gone missing. So, Mr. Armstrong, let's turn your question around. What were you doing in Scotts-dell?"

"Following Skye," he said. "What girl?"

She shook her head. At that moment, a noise erupted from the monitor receiver still clasped in her left hand. Nathan's amplified cries jarred Lara down to her bones.

Bill Armstrong's gaze darted to the monitor and back to her face. She immediately clicked it off.

"Don't look so nervous," he said with a smile that ratcheted up her unease. "I know you have a baby."

Nathan's cries wafted down the stairs behind her. "I have to go—"

He held up both hands as though disowning his previous attempts to detain her. "I know you and Skye are married. I found out about it at the courthouse. And now I know you came back to town with his kid. How about that? He kills my son and a year later, he has one of his own." He lowered his voice to a whisper. "Now, I ask you, is that fair?"

His voice and the sudden passion in his eyes terri-fied her. It came to Lara that he was teetering on the edge of control. She took an instinctive step back, her spine tingling with alarm.

"Has Skye started carrying a gun again, do you know? I understand killing my boy kind of shook him up and he stopped packing. Hard to believe he's willing to leave you and his kid with no protection, but I guess that's how it is with some men."

"What are you saying?" she snapped, anger replacing some of the fear. "Are you threatening us?"

"'Course not," Armstrong said. "I know you got shot a couple of nights ago, that's all. The night Jason Briggs was hurt. How are you feeling by the way? Is your arm mending okay?"

This time she managed to slam the door in his face and click the lock. She stared down the hall toward the kitchen. Had Myra locked that door when she left?

Should she call Brady? Should she pack Nathan into her rental car and leave town?

As she stood in the foyer, racked with fear and indecision, Nathan's cries grew increasingly pathetic.

She had to make a decision. Any decision.

No, she had to make the *right* decision.

BRADY DROVE AWAY from the Wylie house. His growing sense of unease hadn't been soothed by Lucinda Wylie's near hysteria.

He'd been a father for less than two days, at least as far as knowing about it went. He'd spent precious few moments with his son. The child couldn't speak and yet already, Brady found his thoughts straying to him over and over again.

All this newfound understanding made Bill Armstrong's loss all the more real to Brady. No wonder a year wasn't enough time to mitigate the pain. How much time would be enough? A thousand years? A million?

He headed out to the Good Neighbors house. His foreman was excellent, but there were some big decisions coming up that needed Brady's input. He and the foremen settled on a couple of sturdy wooden chairs out back under the trees, the river gurgling nearby, while they ironed out details for the coming week. When that was done, Brady got back in his truck and paused, unsure what to do next. Go back to Lara's house?

No. He suspected she'd want to hash out visiting rights and financial aid, and he suspected that would lead to talk of the inevitable divorce.

He couldn't face it, not right now. Maybe never.

He'd taken a cursory look at Lara's neighbor's front yard before they drove to Scottsdell that morning. He'd found no clues as to who had tried to run him down the night before. It hadn't rained in two and a half months and the neighbor wasn't big on sprinklers, hence he'd found no tire imprints even if he had the resources to take a cast and compare them to Armstrong's truck. A few broken branches didn't point any helpful fingers, either. And the neighbor, who'd come outside to see what Brady was doing, hadn't seen a thing the night before, just heard the engine.

Brady headed home.

The phone inside the house started ringing as he inserted the key in the lock. It hardly ever rang, there were times when he wondered why he even kept a landline. Concerned it might be Lara with a problem, he snatched it off the base on the fifth ring.

A male voice, deeper than Brady remembered, hearty, full of life. "Hey, big brother!"

Brady dropped his keys on the counter and hooked a stool with the toe of his boot, pulling it close. Over the last decade, Garrett had called for one reason and one reason only: he needed help. Perching on the edge of the stool, Brady said, "I can't believe my ears."

"Yeah, I know, it's been a while."

"How are you? Where are you?"

"Actually, I'm in Reno."

Brady frowned as he said, "Why Reno?" *Please, not for the gambling,* Brady added to himself. He'd never known Garrett to be a gambler, but he hadn't heard from his younger brother for three years and three years was enough time for all sorts of bad habits to emerge. Gambling meant debt, which no doubt explained this call.

Garrett said, "I got married a couple of years ago."

"No kidding."

A slight pause was followed by, "It didn't work out. Tiffany decided she wanted to be a showgirl. She moved to Reno so I followed."

"You followed a woman?" Brady said. "That doesn't sound like you."

Garrett's voice took on an edge of sarcasm as he said, "Yeah, right. I'm the one who usually leaves, is that what you're saying?"

Brady didn't answer. He'd been thinking exactly that. Garrett's unwritten manifesto was simple: get involved with someone, make a mess of it, leave. Run away. Let someone else pick up the pieces. Avoid pain. *Like you have room to talk?* his subconscious whispered.

Garrett added, "I didn't follow Shelly. I followed Megan."

"Ah."

"Megan is my daughter, Brady. A two-year-old doll. Tiffany is using my child support to subsidize her new dream job while my little girl spends her time with a grandmother who isn't too thrilled about being a babysitter. I was working at a casino, trying to put something away to fight for full custody, when the comptroller slash bigwig VP hired me to be a body-guard for his wife. The money is a lot better."

Brady could hardly believe his ears. Garrett sounded mature and focused. He said, "That sounds great." He mentally reviewed his finances, wondering how much Garrett would ask for, how much he could spare.

"Brady?"

"Yeah, I'm here. Listen, how much do you need?" He hadn't meant it to come out quite so abruptly.

"What do you mean?"

"Money to tide you over."

Icy silence followed by, "I guess I earned that."

Brady, realizing his gaffe, said, "Hey, I'm sorry. I just figured—"

"It's okay. I've lost count of how many times you've bailed me out of trouble over the years. But not any-more. The reason I'm calling is because of Dad."

"What about him?"

"I've been trying to reach him for three days but he doesn't answer his phone."

"He's probably on a bender."

"Spoken like the cop you've always been even before you put on that uniform," Garrett said. When Brady didn't respond, Garrett added, "Last time I spoke to him was a month ago and he swore he'd quit. When did you see him?"

Marveling that Garrett would actually believe their father after all the broken promises, Brady admitted it had been a couple of months. He didn't include the in-formation that the sighting had been at a distance, him walking down the street, glancing through the open door of one of the riverside taverns, their father sprawled at the bar, a half-empty shot glass in front of him.

"Will you go by his house?" Garrett asked. "Today?"
One more pointless thing to do. "Sure."

"And call me back at this number?"

"Yes."

He wrote down his brother's number and soon after hung up. He snagged the keys again and opened the door.

Lara stood on the step, Nathan in her arms. Brady was so shocked to find her standing there with one hand raised to knock that for a long count, he just stared at her.

Lowering her hand, she spoke without looking at his face. "I have to talk to you."

There was that tone of voice again. Determined, tense. She was getting ready to tell him she was leaving town and they had to talk *now*.

"I have to drive over to my father's house," he said, relieved he had a legitimate excuse for leaving. "Garrett called. He's worried Dad hasn't answered the phone in a few days. I told him I'd call him back, so I better go. We'll hook up later—"

"I'll drive you," she said.

"You don't want to go to my father's house—"

She met his gaze. "Yes, I do. I..." She shook her head and looked away. His heart lurched with concern.

"What's happened since we got back from Scottsdell?" he said, keeping his hands to himself though his instinct was to grab her. "Something is wrong."

"It's nothing. Well, maybe it's something. I don't know. I'm not sure what to do."

He ached to wrap his arms around her. "Just tell me."

"Let's take care of your father first. We've got so much to discuss. But not like this."

"You could wait here."

"No. I want to go with you."

"We'll take your car," he said, adding, "I'll drive."

LARA KNEW where Brady grew up, she'd driven by the house a time or two when they first met. She also knew he very seldom, if ever, went back to that house. She'd run into his father a time or two, but he hadn't been part of the formal wedding plans, he hadn't attended the rehearsal dinner or the shower or any of the other social activities preceding the "big day." The big day that never happened.

Caught up in these thoughts, she glanced over at Brady. He had one of the world's truly great profiles. Strong, well-defined features, lips bordering on chiseled, cheekbones angular, the dark slash of his brows framing the incredible depths of his eyes. He looked preoccupied. Did he care more about his father than he was willing to admit, even to himself?

She tucked her hands beneath her thighs to quell the rampant desire to slide her fingers across the seat, to rest her hand on his thigh as she'd done in the past. Her body longed to bend beneath his. Erotic thoughts hit her fast and hard, leaving her rattled. Maybe the fear Bill Armstrong had awakened with his insinuations caused this pounding desire to have sex with the one man she knew would move the world to protect Nathan.

Was that what she was feeling? Some kind of primal instinct to mate with her protector, to bond him to her and her child?

"How was Garrett?" she asked. She had to get her mind away from Brady's face and body and the magic of his hands, the safety of his arms. She couldn't talk about Bill Armstrong right that moment, this wasn't the time, it could wait until the trip back. Surely Brady's younger brother provided a safe alternate conversation.

He shrugged before saying, "He actually seemed more together than I've ever heard him sound. Maybe he's finally growing up."

"Why do you say that?"

He spared her a quick glance. "He didn't call because he needed bailing out of anything. He's either getting a divorce or already has one, I'm not sure which."

"I didn't know he was married," she said, though of course she wouldn't have known. Garrett had left Riverport after high-school graduation and according to Brady, never looked back.

"And he has a two-year-old daughter."

She smiled. "Really? What did he say when you told him you have a son?"

He cast her another quick look before mumbling, "I don't think I mentioned Nathan."

Narrowing her eyes, she said, "Did you tell him about us? About me?"

"What about you?" he said, staring straight ahead. "That you married me or that you're leaving me?"

"Either one."

"No."

"About the shooting? About quitting the force?"

"No," he said.

She sensed his hackles rising. It was okay to free her hands now, the intense longing to touch him had passed.

Brady's attention was drawn out the side window for a moment and Lara followed his gaze to see a police car parked behind a blue compact. Tom James was leaning down, looking in the window, talking to the driver, a kid Lara vaguely recognized from the teen center days. Tom looked up in time to notice them and nodded slightly as he kept talking to the kid.

"Someone is going to have a lot of explaining to do tonight when they get home and their parents find out they got a ticket," Lara said.

"If they get a ticket. Tom believes in second chances." He glanced at her as he said that.

Did he want a second chance, is that what he was saying? Could she afford to give him one? Could she afford the devastation in her own life if he failed to change? Could she go through all that again?

He turned into a driveway of a very nondescript house whose curtains were drawn. The plants in the front had dried up and died. He parked the car and pulled the parking brake, then turned to face her.

"What do you expect out of me?"

"I don't expect anything," she said in a soft voice, with a backward glance at Nathan asleep in his car seat.

Brady looked at the slumbering baby, too, and lowered his voice. "Yes, you do. You're obviously annoyed I didn't tell Garrett about you and Nathan. On the other hand, you can't wait to leave town and take my boy away from me. Plus, one of these days, you'll find someone new and give Nathan a brand-new stepfather and I'm supposed to brag about this mess to my long-lost brother? I'm supposed to feel good about all this?"

She couldn't bear to meet his gaze, to meet his pain. Every single thing he said was true.

"The trouble is, you don't talk to anyone about anything," she finally murmured. "You set impossible goals of perfection for yourself. You don't trust anyone to love you despite—"

He held up a hand. "Please, honey, no therapy. Not right now. You haven't said what you came to say. Get it over with."

"What do you mean?"

"You're leaving, right?"

"Yes."

"And yet that doesn't explain why you looked so spooked a few minutes ago."

She bit her lip. "I know it doesn't. Brady, do you still have a gun?"

He stared at her for a count of ten. "Yes," he finally said.

"Is it true you don't carry it?"

"I'm a civilian," he said. "How many civilians do you know who carry guns?"

She looked down at her hands as he heaved a sigh. If she kept annoying him like this, he'd stop trying to get close to her.

"Listen," he said, "I've got to go in there and find out what's going on. Stay here and wait."

"I'll go with you—"

"Please, Lara, just stay here. Let me handle this."

And there it was in a nutshell. He wanted to "handle" his father, he wanted to "handle" her. He just didn't know how to do both at the same time. She said, "I could help, Brady."

"No," he said, casting her a miserable look. He walked across the dead grass and knocked on the door. After a minute or two, he tried the handle. The door opened and Brady disappeared inside the house, the door closing behind him.

So, true to form, he'd tucked her away in the car while he saw to his father. That was his standard operating plan: this person and problem here, that person and problem there, never mix them up, don't chance things getting out of control.

A movement on the street behind her caught her attention and she turned in time to see a black truck pull up against the curb across the street. The driver turned and stared through his back window.

Bill Armstrong!

How had he known to come here?

Two nights before, she'd sat in a car with Jason Briggs as a bullet tore through the rear window. Her arm, as though prodded by the memory of the second bullet, the one that had torn into her flesh, throbbed anew. Her face went clammy, her mouth dry. With shaking fingers, she unbuckled her seat belt and got out of the car, unable to even contemplate sitting there like a clay pigeon at a shooting range. She opened the rear door and fumbled with the seat belt holding Nathan's carrier in place, then swooped it and him up. She walked across the dry grass, resisting the urge to glance across the street, opened the front door without knocking and walked straight into the shelter of the house.

And into chaos. An unbelievable clutter of newspapers, bottles, cans, plates of half-eaten food and discarded clothing covered every horizontal surface. It looked as though the house had vomited its contents onto itself.

Plus, the smell. Rotting food. Unwashed bodies. Sickness. It hit her like a fist.

Was this how Brady and Garrett had grown up? In a sty like this? No wonder Brady valued order.

She stopped in her tracks and called, "Brady?"

He stepped out of a bedroom down the hall and

walked toward her. Her stomach unclenched an iota at the solid, real sight of him.

"What's wrong?" he said as he picked his way through the debris.

She stared at his face for a moment. At the despair in his eyes. The sudden stoop of his square shoulders.

"Lara? What's wrong?"

"Nothing," she said, scrambling for a plausible excuse for showing up in a house where it was clear she wasn't wanted.

"It got hot in the car and I thought maybe I could help in here. I'm a trained counselor, remember. I can help you and your father open a dialogue about—"

"He's not here," Brady interrupted, hitching his hands on his waist and surveying the mess. "I don't know," he added. "Maybe he's buried under all this crap. Let's get out of here." His gaze dropped to Nathan, his voice grew tender. He took the carrier from her. "Asleep or not, I don't want the little guy exposed to this filth."

They stepped out onto the porch together. Lara's gaze darted across the street. Bill Armstrong was gone.

As Brady closed and locked the door, a police car pulled in behind her rental.

Chapter Eight

As Tom got out of the car, Brady glanced up and down the street. Not a single neighbor peered around an open door or through an unshuttered window. Apparently the arrival of a police unit at 322 Court Way didn't arouse much curiosity anymore.

"What's up?" Brady asked.

Tom smiled at Lara and tickled Nathan's cheek. Glancing back at Brady, he said, "A call just came over the radio. The owner of the River Rat reported a disturbance. Chief Dixon was on his way home and took the call. I saw you pass a minute ago and figured you were driving over here. Do you want to go down there with me?"

"Why would I—"

"It's your dad."

Brady took a deep breath. He glanced at Lara, his gaze fell to Nathan.

"Don't worry about us," Lara said. Did her voice tremble? He glanced into her eyes but she looked away again. What was going on?

"Are you sure you're okay?" he asked her.

"Of course," she added brightly, reaching for Nathan's carrier. "I'll catch up with you later."

Tom tapped his watch. "If you're coming…"

"Yeah, okay, I won't be long, Lara."

His conscience whispered to him as Lara walked toward the rental. *You're relieved fate has once again intervened to cut short the farewell conversation.* When had he become such a coward?

"You going back to your mother's house?" he called.

She turned, met his gaze and shrugged.

"You won't leave town," he said.

"Not tonight," she said. "Go. Don't worry."

He settled into the passenger seat and Tom wasted no time backing out of the driveway and speeding off.

It was the first time since the night he shot Billy Armstrong that Brady had been inside a squad car. The memories it brought back choked him with regret. For the millionth time, he wished Billy and Jason Briggs had chosen the next night to swipe a car and steal beer. By then, he would have been honeymooning on a beach in Hawaii. Billy would probably still be alive, Brady and Lara would be living as man and wife, Jason might not be laid out in the hospital.

"You happen to know how the Briggs boy is doing?" Brady asked Tom as he turned onto River Front Street.

"The same. Still in a coma, not talking, but I doubt he knows who plugged him."

"How about you guys? Do the cops have any leads? Tire tracks, bullet casings, witnesses?"

"The doctor dug a 30–08 out of the boy. That bullet could have come out of any deer rifle in the county or from an assault weapon. We're looking for stolen. No witnesses besides you."

"Did Bill Armstrong have an alibi?"

"Not much of one. Said he was driving around. Chief Dixon said he saw him."

"Dixon saw him, huh? I don't suppose Armstrong admitted stopping by the Kirk house to lob a rock through the parlor window?"

"Claimed he didn't know what I was talking about. I'll keep an eye on him."

It was on the tip of his tongue to tell Tom about the incident in front of the Kirk house early that morning, the one that had him dodging into a hedge, but what was the point? Instead he said, "How about Karen Wylie?"

"How about her? A runaway. I guess her mom's been calling Chief Dixon. Does he have you to thank for that?"

"Probably. I talked to a couple of people in Scotts-dell today. A homeless guy saw her get off the bus with a suitcase, a cranky old woman who lives across the street from the old warehouse down the street saw her walking away with a man about my size."

"Oh, brother, I hope the chief doesn't get wind of that. He'd love to pin all this on you."

"Tom, I'm not that unusual a size. Bill Armstrong is as tall as I am. A little heavier maybe. For that matter, so are you and Dixon and the guy at the gas station. Besides, why would I run off with a seventeen-year-old kid?"

Tom spared him a wry glance. "Seventeen isn't a kid, Brady. You have an alibi for yesterday afternoon?"

"I was driving around Riverport trying to find the girl. Her mother was coming apart."

Tom shook his head. "You get any names from these witnesses?"

"No. The woman won't be hard to find. The guy was standing on a corner across from the bus station holding a sign begging for gas money for a car he doesn't have. He might be gone by now."

"I'll write this up when I get to the station. Might as well have someone go out and question those two tomorrow," Tom said as he slowed down. The chief's unmarked car was parked in front of the River Rat. As Brady got out of the car, he steeled himself for what was coming.

The River Rat was no stranger to drunks or cops. Built fifty years earlier and mucked out every decade or so, it defied health codes. It was the kind of place for serious drinkers, no party-going yuppies need apply.

A call squawked on the squad car radio. As Tom moved to take it, Brady said, "If you have to go, don't worry, I'll get him home in a cab."

Tom nodded as he leaned in and grabbed the mike.

This early on an August evening, the joint was blessedly free of crowds. Besides the bartender, Chief Dixon and Brady's father, there were just two bleary-eyed older guys down at the end of the bar.

Brady's father sat on a stool, weathering Dixon's hissed remonstrations. It was hard to believe this wasted man had once fought in Korea, had once driven a logging truck, had wooed and won the heart of a beautiful woman.

Charles Skye. Hair graying and sparse body, too thin in places and too thick in others. Clothes that needed washing, face that needed shaving, expression slack. The kind of man more at home in a gutter than on a sidewalk.

The kind of man for whom Brady had always felt little more than contempt.

But watching Dixon berate his father aroused a curious sensation in the pit of Brady's stomach. Forced to name it, he'd have to go with *pity*. For the first time he felt pity for his old man.

Unnoticed by Dixon or his father, Brady caught the proprietor's eye and leaned across the bar. Harry Pie was about the same age as the other two men, and like them had spent his life in Riverport. "My father was causing trouble?" Brady asked.

Harry shook his shaved head. "No. Couple of punks came in and started giving him grief. They left as soon as I called the cops. Your dad didn't do nothing but sit there and take it. I expected him to throw a few punches, but not tonight."

Ignoring Dixon's glare, Brady approached his father. "Come on, Dad," he said, laying a hand on the older man's shoulder. "Time to call it a night."

His father looked up at him with eyes diluted by years of vodka transfusions.

Chief Dixon turned his belligerence on Brady. "I'm damn tired of you getting in my face, Skye."

"Running into you isn't my idea of a good time, either," Brady said.

"I heard about you going to Scottsdell today."

How had he heard that quickly? It implied a tail of some kind. Brady said, "It was a nice day for a drive."

"Listen to me. The Wylie girl ran off, clear and simple. Now you got her mother all riled up, calling us, demanding we find her kid and haul her home. You know it doesn't work like that."

Ah, Karen Wylie's mother had demanded action. Brady said, "I don't know how it works. Like you keep telling me, I'm not a cop."

"And don't you forget it. Now, get your old man out of here before I throw his ass in jail."

Brady's father didn't appear interested in the conversation. He'd stopped looking at Brady and instead studied the empty shot glass on the counter as though desire could fill it.

Brady gently pulled his father to his feet. He looked over his old man's head and said, "What did he ever do to you, Dixon? Why do you hate him?"

Dixon chewed on his cheek for a second. Brady would have bet a bundle the man was dying for a cigarette.

With a barman's nose for gossip, Harry Pie moseyed along the bar until he stood opposite them. Pretending to wipe down the counter with a damp rag, he said, "Didn't your Dad ever tell you about your mother?"

Dixon cast Harry an if-looks-can-kill frown and said, "Never you mind, Harry."

Brady's dad looked up. "Theresa?" he said, glancing around as though her ghost might have stopped in for a nightcap.

"Don't you even say her name," Dixon spat.

Theresa Skye had died driving drunk twelve years earlier. Brady didn't even know Dixon knew his mother past recognizing her as Charlie Skye's wife. It stunned him to hear Dixon's distress at hearing Charles Skye speak her name.

Dixon glared at Brady and added, "Get your old man sober. Keep him that way."

Sure, Brady thought. *That'll happen.*

As Dixon stomped out of the place, Harry Pie wiped a nonexistent spot from the bar and said, "Dix, Charlie, Theresa and I all went to school together. Did you know that?"

"I guess," Brady said. He tried to move his father a step closer to the door. The man was thin as a reed but oddly bottom heavy, as though all his weight had pooled in his feet.

"Theresa married Dix right out of high school," Harry added. Brady stopped trying to budge his dad and looked at Harry.

"What did you say?"

"Your dad went away to join the navy. When he got home, Theresa left Dix and married Charlie. Dix never got over it."

Stunned, Brady mumbled, "My mother was once married to Chief Dixon?"

"'Course, he wasn't a chief then," Harry said, rubbing a spot on the bar with his cloth. "Dix couldn't go into the service because of some sleepwalking thing. I guess he propositioned a thirteen-year-old girl down the block, leastwise, that was the rumor going around, so Theresa threw him out and married Charlie. I think Dix is working on wife number three now. Anyway, it was all very hush-hush."

"Chief Dixon propositioned a kid?"

"That's what your dad said a long time ago. I don't have any way of knowing if it's the truth or not. I can't believe no one ever told you about this."

Brady looked at his father's face. His old man blinked and trotted out a belch. Again, Brady felt a twinge of pity.

He didn't try to explain to Harry Pie that by the time Brady was old enough to care about things like his parents' pasts, both had been lost in a bottle.

APPARENTLY, CHARLES SKYE had been more aware of what happened at the bar than he'd let on.

"Dix is a jerk," he said in a garbled, slurred voice as Brady shoveled him into a taxi. Charlie Skye had lost his license years ago and usually staggered home under his own steam or caught a ride. When Brady first became a cop, he'd actually tried to be at the bar at closing time so he could give his father a lift. That had ended when his father socked him in the eye and told him to mind his own business.

"Yeah," Brady said, giving the driver his father's address.

"Thought he owned Theresa," the older man continued, pulling at his pants as he spoke as though the cloth burned his skin. "Even after she left. Tried to get her back."

"I didn't know they were married," Brady said.

His father grew very still. He finally looked up at Brady and mumbled, "You were the good one. You were the one who answered the door."

The one who kept the cops and the neighbors and the school officials away, Brady thought to himself.

I was the enabler in my family. I was the glue.

Well, what choice had he had? Someone had to see that there was food around and that bills got paid and Garrett didn't rot in detention after ditching classes day after day.

"Your brother got in trouble all the time," Brady's father said, his voice lower now and close to a snore. He jerked and flung a hand up and said, "Where's Theresa?"

"Dead," Brady said. They'd had this conversation, like all the others, a hundred times, a thousand times. "She's gone, Dad."

"Dix's a jerk," his father repeated, bookending his conversation, and then his chin slumped onto his bony chest.

Brady managed to pay the driver and wrangle his father into the house where he deposited him on a semiclean chair while he went into the bedroom, changed the sheets and started the shower. A half hour later, his dad tucked in bed and dead to the world, he called Garrett.

"Sorry to take so long getting back to you," he said.

"Dad down on River Front Street?"

"Yeah. He's home now. Listen, Garrett. There are some things I need to get cleared away up here and then I thought I might come down your way and visit you in Reno. It's been a while since we really talked."

What had caused him to say that? *Lara.* She'd gotten under his skin. He filled the silence by adding, "If this isn't a good time—"

"I think it's a great idea," Garrett said. "I've been thinking of coming up that way, myself. I'd like to show Riverport to Megan."

"Let's give it a few weeks and talk again," Brady suggested. "We'll figure out who goes where."

Brady worked off the tight feeling in his chest by scouring his father's house, loading the dishwasher and dumping empty bottles into the recycling bin. He hadn't revealed their mother's first marriage to Garrett. That was news better left for a face-to-face meeting. And they hadn't talked about treatment plans for their dad because they'd been down that road a dozen times before.

He knew Garrett understood, as he did, that there would be no long-term help until Charles Skye really wanted it. Down deep. Down in his gut. Down where he kept his pain. If alcoholism was a disease, then it had to be fought like one and not surrendered to. Until then, he might sober up for a few days or even weeks, he might swear to turn his life around, but sooner or later he'd seek refuge where he knew he could find it.

At three-thirty in the morning, Brady found his father's car keys and went out to the garage to see if the old sedan still ran. Wonder of wonders, it turned over at the first try. He drove himself home and as he walked to his apartment around in the back, he happened to see a car parked at the end of the row behind his neighbor's piano-delivery truck. Lara's rental, Nathan's car seat abandoned in the backseat.

He walked quickly around to his door only to discover a broken pane of glass by the lock, patched now with a piece of wood pounded into place with a dozen nails from the inside. That explained how she got in. The door was now locked again and he opened it.

The apartment was pitch-black. He hit the switch on the wall. Nothing happened. Odd, and considering everything, a tad alarming. He stepped inside. Before he could turn the light on, he ran into a pile of pots and pans that clanged and rattled to the floor as he scrambled to catch them.

What was going on?

Why had Lara set a trap and why didn't the noise of it clamoring to the ground bring her scampering into the room? He tried the light switch, but nothing happened. Using the tiny flashlight on his key ring, he stepped around the mess. The fuse box was in the kitchen. Only the switch for the entry lights had been thrown and he reset it.

He found her on his bed. Not only on his bed, but on his side of the bed. Fully clothed, stretched out on top of the sheet, all legs and blond hair and delicate tan, as smooth as a centerfold and a hundred times more appealing because she had once been his.

And would be again.

Standing there, staring at her in the weak light of his tiny flashlight, he made a promise to himself and to her.

And to his son, who had apparently kicked aside a blue baby blanket and now wore nothing but a diaper. He lay beside her, occupying an amazing amount of real estate smack in the middle of the mattress. His small, half-clad body looked so impossibly vulnerable that Brady's heart all but stopped beating. He flicked on a lamp and turned off the flashlight.

He moved to rouse Lara but stopped himself. She must be exhausted. How else to explain being nervous enough to set a trap but sleepy enough to nod off and miss the sound of it springing? Was there any reason to wake her now?

Maybe he should ease her farther down on the bed, cover her though the room was warm. She'd be more comfortable without her shoes—

Which would mean he'd have to cup her smooth, bare calves in his hands, unstrap her sandals. He'd have to lift her shoulders, reposition her head. He could almost feel the silky strands of her hair sliding between his fingers…

No, he wouldn't touch her. He wouldn't torture himself.

He rubbed the bridge of his nose with thumb and forefinger. His leg hurt where he'd gouged his knee the night before. His heart felt heavy and way too big for his chest. He turned around and stared at Lara and Nathan as the seconds ticked off on the alarm clock.

Was there any danger in just catching a few hours' sleep before finding out what was going on?

He walked to his dresser. His keys, with the flashlight attached, were still in his hand. He found the right key and used it to open the locked drawer on top.

The Glock seemed to glow in its holster. He stared at it, even reached for it. But his fingers stopped short of touching the damn thing, and he shut and locked the drawer again. He left the lamp burning on the dresser, then headed to the closet for a blanket and pillow. He'd settle for a few hours on the sofa.

Wait. This was his house, his wife, his child, his bed. For what was left of the night, they could all just share. He stripped down to his boxers and slipped beneath the sheet on Nathan's far side.

His weight hitting the mattress jostled Lara. She sat bolt upright with a gasp, eyes flying open. Grabbing her chest with her hand, relief flooded her face as he whispered her name.

Tears glistened in her eyes, but they didn't fall. He'd noticed the new Lara didn't cry.

Nathan whimpered, then relaxed once again into sleep. Lara pulled the baby blanket up around the baby's frail shoulders as Brady rolled onto his side and watched her.

What had she done with the ring he'd given her? She didn't need the money, so he knew she wouldn't have sold or hawked it, not yet at least, not until she remarried, maybe, and his ring became a memory of a marriage she wanted to forget.

Her ring, her husband.

"How's your father?" she said at last.

"Sleeping it off. Why are you here, Lara? Why did you break in and booby-trap the front hall? What happened today?"

"Bill Armstrong came to see me."

He took a deep breath and started to roll off the bed.

She reached across Nathan and caught his arm, snapping her hand back at once. "No," she said softly.

He stared at her. "Why the hell not?"

"He didn't really do anything."

"That's why you came here earlier today," he said. "You were afraid but you didn't tell me. You wouldn't tell me."

"I guess I thought you had other things on your mind. And then Bill drove by your father's place. I just got spooked. So after you left with Tom, I decided to come here because Myra was staying with her sister for the night, and I couldn't stand the thought of being in my mother's big house alone."

"And you haven't seen Armstrong since he drove by my father's place?"

"No. He said he came to your apartment earlier in the day, but I got the feeling he didn't think you lived here anymore so I thought it might be safe. I'm sorry about your door and the pans—"

"Don't," he said, his gut twisting at the thought of her fear. He'd put her off, he'd left her. He'd been relieved to have an excuse to avoid confrontation.

"I'm the one who's sorry," he said.

"I looked for your gun."

He kept a smile to himself as he said, "You were going to shoot Bill Armstrong?"

"If I had to," she said.

"You don't know how to shoot. You would never let me teach you anything more than how to click off the safety."

They stared at each other. He wasn't sure what she was feeling. He was suffering a major case of guilt and inadequacy.

She finally yawned and rubbed her temple, then slipped back down in the bed, resetting her head on the pillow. "Can we finish talking about this in the morning? I'm so tired I hurt."

"It is morning."

"You're here now," she whispered as her eyes drifted shut.

He stared at her a few moments longer, memories of making love to her stampeding through his head, galloping south where they wreaked havoc on his libido.

He lay awake for a long time.

Chapter Nine

As Nathan slept the next morning, Lara sat cross-legged on her side of the bed. Brady propped his shoulders against the headboard. She told him everything she could remember about Bill Armstrong's visit the day before. He listened with his usual intensity, reading between the lines, his expression growing increasingly murderous.

Eventually, Nathan woke up and they moved to Brady's small kitchen. He cleaned up the pots and pans while she fed the baby.

In retrospect, her behavior the night before seemed way over the top. How had she allowed herself to get so spooked?

Flat, dead eyes floated in front of her. Oh, yeah. That's how.

Brady finally sat down, ignoring the folded newspaper at his elbow and playing at eating cold cereal. She knew he was upset and was trying to figure out what he should do next. He threw occasional glances at her and Nathan, his expression so tender it almost hurt.

How could something that at times seemed so right, at other times seem so wrong? How could she change him?

You can't, you fool. The cost of loving Brady Skye is

allowing him to set the limits. Allowing him to keep things to himself, to brood when he needs to, to let him draw lines around everything and everyone and keep it all separate and safe. Can you spend your life like that?

No. And that meant getting out of Brady's apartment where the fantasy of them being a family tore at her heart.

When Nathan started cooing, she handed him to Brady's outstretched hands and poured them both more coffee. She'd brought no clean clothes so there was nothing to do after breakfast but go back to her mother's house. She said, "Brady, about this divorce."

He looked up at her, his expression frozen.

"Now that you know about Nathan, we can go ahead with the proceedings."

"Lucky us," he said.

She ignored his remark. "I don't really want to move back to Riverport, at least not right now, but on the other hand, I do want you to be part of Nathan's life."

"Just not part of yours."

"Brady, please. Don't make this harder—"

"Sorry," he said, casting her a dark look, the kind that despite its surliness reminded her what it was like to be pulled into his demanding arms, his gentleness tinged with need, his giving, his taking, all of it wrapped up in the heart-stopping power that surged through his body into hers like a freight train.

"I see no reason to make this easy," he added.

"What do you mean?"

"I don't want you to leave."

"That's what I'm trying to say. I'll move back unless you want to move north."

"You mean up to Seattle?"

"Yes. I imagine they need cops up that way the same way—"

"No."

"Brady—"

"I won't carry a gun again," he said. "But all this is a moot point because I have decided to win you back."

She heard Nathan cry. Naps were like that sometimes—they could be ten minutes or two hours, you just never knew. She got to her feet and stared down at Brady. "We've been through this."

"Just give me a few more days," he said. "There's a lot at stake here, you know."

"But it's pointless."

"Shall I go get Nathan or do you want to get him?"

He was putting her off—again. She walked quickly down the hall. Nathan lay on Brady's bed, halfhearted cries alternating with hiccups. She picked him up, threw a clean diaper over her shoulder to catch spit-ups and soothed him, walking back down the hall, determined to come to some conclusion with Brady.

Her new cell phone rang as she entered the kitchen again. Brady turned from the sink where he'd been rinsing out his bowl and reached out for Nathan, plopping down in his chair as Lara dug in her bag for her cell phone. She didn't recognize the displayed number except that it was local.

"Hello?" she said as she leaned against the counter.

"Is this Miss Kirk?" a young female voice asked.

"Yes, it is."

"My name is Nicole. Nicole Stevens. Do you remember me?"

A vague image of a small girl with waist-length glistening black hair floated into Lara's mind. "Did you used to come into the teen center?"

The relief in the girl's voice was audible. "Yeah, I did. I was a friend of Sara Armstrong's."

And Karen Wylie. The three of them had hung out together. Lara glanced at Brady who had caught her tone of voice and was looking at her. Lara said, "I remember. How are you?"

"Okay. I guess. I was wondering if I could talk to you."

"Of course you can talk to me," Lara said, her gaze linked to Brady's. "What can I do for you?"

"I am also a friend of Karen Wylie's, Miss Kirk." The girl lowered her voice. "Karen ran away day before yesterday. Her mom said you talked to her before she left."

"Yes, I did."

"That's why I want to talk to you. But not on the phone. Will you meet me tomorrow?"

"How about today?"

"No." The voice got even softer. "I'm off work today and I have…plans."

"Okay. How about the coffee shop?"

"No. Someplace more private."

"You mean someplace with fewer people?" Lara said, her mind immediately leaping to Jason Briggs's call a few days earlier. Hadn't he made the same request? But this time she'd have Brady with her. No reason to tell Nicole that, but Lara sure as hell wasn't going alone. "Like where?" she added.

"I babysit a couple of kids. They like to go to the park, to that new play-structure thing, do you know what I'm talking about?"

"Yes," Lara said.

"There's a bench off to the side."

"Okay. What time?"

"Three-thirty?"

"Okay." Lara paused for a second before adding, "Karen's mom told me you and Karen used to like to go to Sara's house. She said Sara's father was like a dad to all you guys."

Nicole didn't respond, but Brady's eyebrows shot up his forehead.

"Yeah, I guess," Nicole said after several seconds. Her voice held a new edge of wariness.

Afraid she was in the process of scaring Nicole off, Lara said, "I was just thinking how nice it was you were all so close."

Strained silence.

"Sara was a sweet girl," Lara added.

Finally, a soft, "Miss Kirk, let's keep the meeting just between us, okay?"

A chill ran up Lara's spine. "Sure."

Nicole disconnected.

"What was that all about?" Brady asked.

Lara set the phone down and returned to her seat across from Brady. She fooled around with her mug of cold coffee before saying, "You're going to think I'm nuts, but there's something odd going on. I had a lot of time to think yesterday, you know. I mean, does Bill Armstrong strike you as the cuddly father-figure type?"

"No," Brady said, using the diaper to wipe a trickle of drool from Nathan's chin.

"Me, neither."

"But Armstrong's had a horrible year."

"True. I'm just going to say this. I don't have any proof, it's just a thought but it won't go away."

"Go for it."

"What if Bill Armstrong is a child molester?"

Brady's forehead furrowed. "How did you ever reach that conclusion?"

"Bear with me. First his daughter kills herself without leaving a note. That seems odd. Teenage girls like drama, and if she had something horrible enough in her life to kill herself over, I think she would have left a suicide note. No, before you ask, I don't know what the statistics are, but I did know Sara. She changed right before her death. She got quiet and introspective and started writing long poems. What would cause her to kill herself without a note?"

"Her desire to protect someone?"

"Yes. Like her mother. Like, if her father was molesting her. I wish I knew if she died a virgin."

"She didn't," Brady said. "I saw the autopsy report."

"There you go."

"Honey, lots of sixteen-year-old girls have sex with their boyfriends."

"Right. I just don't recall Sara having a boyfriend. Okay, let's move on to Karen Wylie. Her mother went on and on about Karen's relationship with Bill Armstrong."

"So, obviously he was molesting her, too?"

"Don't laugh at me."

"I'm not laughing."

"And now a third girl wants a private conversation. And when I mentioned Bill Armstrong's name, she grew guarded."

Brady laid Nathan over his lap and gently burped him. "So?"

"So maybe Bill Armstrong met Karen Wylie in Scottsdell."

"Then drove back here in time to threaten you at your mother's house?"

"Maybe he stashed Karen in a motel somewhere. Maybe we need to figure out a way to get to her before it's too late."

"Too late?" He picked Nathan up and cradled him against his broad shoulder, doing all these baby things with an ease that amazed Lara.

"One girl is dead. One is gone," she said. "Another one is on the phone, afraid. She wants to talk to me. So did Jason Briggs. Jason is in the hospital. Doesn't that sound suspicious to you?"

"Yes," he admitted, patting Nathan's back. The baby squirmed and fussed. Brady got to his feet and paced the small room, a movement that quieted Nathan for about ten seconds. "But there's nothing here that is vaguely related to evidence."

"If Bill Armstrong thought news of his perversions were about to be spread, he'd panic. He'd probably do anything to make sure the other girls didn't talk. He'd be ruined—"

"Have you seen him?" Brady said. "He's already ruined."

She smiled. "Are you defending Bill Armstrong?"

He handed her Nathan. "Take your son, he doesn't want me, he wants you. And no, I'm not defending Bill Armstrong."

He sat back down and picked up the local paper, snapping it open. His gaze fell to the headlines as Lara checked Nathan's diaper, then he sat up straighter and slammed the table with an open hand.

The baby, momentarily startled by the gesture, stopped fussing.

"Look," he said, sliding the paper across the table.

A picture of a house fire occupied the space above the fold. The headline screamed, One Life Lost in Scottsdell Inferno.

"This is terrible," Lara mumbled. House fires had always terrified her. She supposed that came from growing up in a three-story Victorian with a mother who thought fire alarms were "ugly."

"Open up the front page," Brady said.

Lara snapped the paper open, which further startled Nathan, who renewed his cries. As she raised him to her shoulder and soothed him, she glanced at the second photo and read, "'Longtime Scottsdell resident, Mrs. Roberta Beaton, wife of late mayor Roscoe Beaton, died in a fire last night that burned her home to the ground.'"

The picture showed the feisty woman they'd spoken to the day before.

"I KILLED HER," Lara said. She'd finally gotten Nathan down for another morning nap and now stood in Brady's living room feeling as though the earth had dropped out from under her feet.

"Of course you didn't," Brady said.

She sat down on the ottoman. "You don't understand. When Bill Armstrong began threatening me, I lashed out. I told him we spoke with a witness who spotted him with Karen Wylie. I was trying to unnerve him. I didn't tell you before because it's embarrassing he got such a rise out of me."

Brady sat down in the chair opposite her. "What did he say?"

"Nothing. No, wait, I didn't mention Karen by name. He asked me what girl I was talking about."

"So we don't know if he followed us there or was already in town—"

"Visiting Karen wherever he stashed her."

Brady ran a hand through his hair. "This is all supposition. And stop blaming yourself. You didn't even know Roberta Beaton's name. You couldn't have told Armstrong which woman you meant."

"If he saw us in Scottsdell, maybe he saw us talking to Mrs. Beaton. It wouldn't take a genius to put two and two together."

Brady was quiet for a second before he said, "You're not the only one who mentioned her. I told Tom. He said he'd inform the detective in charge of Jason's shooting, just in case these things dovetail down the line. That means the whole department—including Bill Armstrong's bother-in-law who works dispatch—knew we'd talked to the woman across from the boarded-up warehouse. Plus, I wouldn't be surprised if Dixon talked to Armstrong."

Lara buried her face in her hands. She couldn't imagine that spunky woman burned to death.

Brady's phone rang. He took the call, uttering very few words before hanging up and returning to Lara. He reached for her hands and pulled her to her feet.

She went into his arms without quibbling. She needed his strength, his big solid body so warm and so real in a world that suddenly seemed full of shadows. His breath on the back of her neck was comforting, his heart beating so close to hers, a balm.

He held her for a long time, their bodies melding together where they touched. She knew allowing this contact was cruel to both of them. It would be so much easier to hate him than to love him.

Would he break his promise and kiss her? She could save him the decision by initiating the kiss herself. Was she ready to do that?

Why? Because she wanted to live with him as his wife or because she felt wretched and scared and wanted the comfort he offered? Being on the taking end of easy comfort always came with a price. Was she prepared to pay it?

She said, "Who was on the phone?"

"Tom," he said, his exhaled breath brushing her ear, sending deep quivering sensations pulsing through her body. She made herself put some distance between them.

He looked down at her with an expression she knew. He had remembered making love to her. He had hoped it would happen again. Hell, despite knowing better, so had she.

He took a deep breath. "The preliminary finding is that the fire was started by Roberta Beaton's kerosene heater igniting a stack of old newspapers. Apparently the old lady never threw anything away. The Scottsdell Police Department said they've been anticipating a tragedy at that address for a decade or more."

"It's all so convenient," Lara said.

"And coincidental," Brady murmured. "I have to go talk to Armstrong. He has to know to stay away from you and Nathan."

"Can't the police—"

"You said he wanted to talk to me yesterday, so I'll go talk to him."

"And if he's behind everything that's happened?"

"You mean Jason's gunshot wound and Karen Wylie's leaving home?"

She nodded.

"He'll continue to come apart at the seams," Brady said. "Sooner or later he'll implode. I just want to make sure he doesn't do it anywhere around you or Nathan."

THE ARMSTRONG HOUSE was only two blocks from the Wylie house. Sandra Armstrong opened the door before Brady even knocked and stood there with no expression on her face. She looked to be about his age with light brown eyes and matching straight hair pulled back with a clip. She wore jean shorts and a white tank, bare feet.

He'd seen her at the inquest into her son's death but not since. Brady wished with all his heart he hadn't come to this house. He'd expected to find Bill. For some reason, he hadn't counted on Sandra.

"He's not here," she said.

He backed away. "I'm sorry I bothered you."

She stared at him for a long time as though on the verge of saying something. He waited as all sorts of things happened behind her eyes.

"My husband's vendetta is tearing him apart," she finally said.

Brady said, "I know."

"He blames you for everything."

Brady knew that, too.

"But that doesn't mean he should be wanting to hurt you in the same way you hurt him."

Brady stopped his retreat and advanced a step. "Do you mean by hurting my son?"

"Hurting your boy won't bring ours back."

"Is he trying to hurt my boy?" Brady said softly.

"He talks about it. It scares me."

It scared her! It was all he could do to keep his voice even as he said, "Maybe if your husband and I could sit down and talk—"

"He won't sit down with you. You killed our Billy."

"I had no choice, Mrs. Armstrong. Please believe me. There was no other option."

"There's always an option," she said, and quietly closed the door.

Always an option? Was she right? As he drove to Lara's house he thought back to the night he shot Billy Armstrong and tried to figure out what else he could have done.

Tom's gun was still in its holster. He'd been talking to Billy about his sister, Sara, trying to calm Billy down. Billy was the one who went off the deep end and reached for a weapon. Billy had upped the stakes. It was just a case of protecting the innocent and in that case, Billy had not been the innocent.

Billy or Tom.

Brady had done what he had to do, what he was sworn to do. And now he would have to live with it and with the fact that there was no proof the boy had ever had a gun, that what Brady had seen wasn't the flash of his watchband distorted by his own fear.

It didn't matter. It was over and he would have to live with it.

But should Nathan have to live with it, too?

LARA STOOD in the doorway of her old bedroom as Brady paced back and forth.

"You have to go," he said. "No argument. Now."

Lara had left Nathan downstairs with Myra. The look the housekeeper had thrown Brady as he dragged Lara up the stairs to pack was one of mixed emotions that still played in Lara's mind. Delight they were arguing, sadness Lara and Nathan seemed to be leaving.

She said, "I'm not going anywhere, Brady."

He dragged her suitcase out of her closet and threw it on the bed. "Yes, you are. You're going to pack up all your stuff and you're going to leave Riverport right now. You're not going to come back. Get your mother to visit you up in Seattle."

"I have to be here to talk to Nicole. Have you forgotten about her?"

"I'll talk to her—"

"She called *me,* Brady. I have to go."

"I don't care about this Nicole, Lara. I care about you and Nathan. I want you both out of Riverport as of yesterday. Just go."

"I thought you were going to win me back," she said, still standing in the doorway. As odd as it seemed, his anxiety had dampened hers.

"Change of plans. Where are the divorce papers? I'll sign them right now."

Was it possible his declaration of the morning had actually reawakened a spark of hope in her heart? She wasn't sure except that it currently seemed in danger of being extinguished, and how could that be if it had never existed in the first place?

Had she made the decision to risk everything without ever acknowledging that decision to herself? She said, "No."

He was piling baby clothes and diapers into the

suitcase. He stopped for a second and looked up at her. "Have you listened to a thing I've said?"

"Yes. Bill Armstrong's wife believes he's on the verge of hurting Nathan." Speaking the words out loud made her stomach churn. She quickly added, "You want us out of town right now."

"That's right," he said, opening the dresser drawer and scooping up a handful of her underwear without giving any indication he saw what he held. "You understand. Now, pack. Please."

"No."

"Why not?" he barked, a satiny pink thong trailing down his arm.

"We're safer here with you to protect us."

"That's very flattering and totally wrong," he said, glancing twice at the underwear as he added it to the growing pile in the suitcase.

"If Armstrong is determined to hurt Nathan, do you really think taking him a hundred miles north will make a difference? You have to figure this out and while you do, Nathan and I will be safe in this big fortress of a house with you standing guard."

"But—"

"And why are you suddenly willing to sign the divorce papers?"

"I want you to get Nathan away from here," he said slowly, as though worried he might have said everything too fast before and she hadn't caught it. "I want you to raise him where everyone who looks at him won't judge him for being a Skye."

"Like your father," she said, gearing up for the old argument.

"No. Like me. I will always be the cop who killed

the unarmed kid. Long after they forget Billy Armstrong's name, they'll remember the name Skye. Long after my father's drunken ways are just a memory, my contribution to the disgrace of bearing the Skye name will still burn bright. Change Nathan's name to Kirk. Get him out of here."

"You could leave Riverport," she said.

He shook his head. "I can't even think about that until this matter is resolved."

She stepped into the room, closed the door, and on second thought locked it. She did not want Myra barging in. She walked to the far side of the bed and sat down next to the suitcase. Patting the mattress on her other side, she said, "Sit down."

He sat beside her but not before glancing at his watch.

"Do you love Nathan?" she asked.

He studied her face for a long time before narrowing his eyes. "You know I do."

"Yes. And your love is what is going to keep him safe. Until this threat is over, until Bill Armstrong stops acting crazy and gets some help, we need to stay together. My taking Nathan away might well escalate things. I can't leave knowing that."

And I can't leave you to bear the brunt of his revenge alone, she added to herself.

He took a deep breath before saying, "You talk about love as though it's some kind of armor."

"Isn't it?" she said, and without thinking, reached up to brush a few dark strands of hair off his forehead. He caught her hand, moved it to his mouth. His lips pressed against the pads of her fingers, sending echoes of passion throughout her body.

"People lose the ones they love all the time," Brady said, his warm breath caressing her palm. "Love can't protect against evil."

"I know," she said, closing her eyes. What was happening? She felt hot and cold at the same time. Felt at peace and yet frightened. Felt like running away and like staying.

She could hear the creaks of the old house as Myra moved around in the kitchen. Brady inched closer; desire resonated in the tiny space between them.

His free hand traveled around her back, his fingers ran lightly under her waistband, down near her tailbone, brushing the rounded curves of her buttocks. It was time to move away from him. It was time to think clearly.

Instead, she arched closer.

Chapter Ten

Her minimal surrender was not lost on Brady whose life force seemed to double in the blink of his deep, dark eyes. She could feel his focus shift from their argument onto her as a woman. His silent realization of the changing stakes was so strong it instantly charged the atmosphere in the room.

She'd always known he regarded her as his. His love, his woman, his wife. Being the center of such desire was hypnotic and she had to guard against it. But her body knew his passion was equaled only by his enthusiasm, and inside she could feel the beginning of the end to reason.

Her heart banged against her ribs as his lips moved close to hers. "Remember your promise," she whispered, as if throwing out a life preserver and hoping one of them had the good sense to grab it.

"I promised I wouldn't kiss you again," he murmured in his sexy, low grumble that skated on the edge of every nerve ending in her back. His hot breath bathed her neck, then he tenderly sucked on her earlobe, sending long-dormant hormones into overdrive.

Maybe just a kiss. Just one. What could it hurt? She

put her hand on his chin and closed her eyes as she guided his mouth to hers.

He turned his face at the last moment, and her lips landed on his cheek. Okay, he had a lot more willpower than she had. Who would have thought that in the end what would save her from her traitorous body would be his common sense?

"I made no promises about not making love to you," he added.

Walk away...

"Come here," he said, sliding off the bed onto his knees, pulling her along so that she landed next to him, on the luxurious carpet.

"What are we doing?" she said very softly.

"What do you think we're doing?" he said, tugging his T-shirt off over his head, exposing his finely toned chest. Without even thinking about it, her fingers sprang to touch him, to stroke his muscles, to delight in the fiery heat of his bronzed skin.

"We shouldn't—" she said, even as her hands dipped down his chest and over his flat belly, brushing the buttons on his jeans and the obvious arousal straining beneath the denim.

He unbuttoned her blouse very slowly, never taking his eyes off her face. Her bra was a front-hooking type and he unhooked it, freeing her breasts, catching the hot mounds in his hands, his gaze dipping, his eyes feverish and hungry.

He licked his lips. The sight of his tongue flicking across his lips made her delirious. "Beautiful," he whispered. "So beautiful."

Maybe one last time, she told herself as he lowered his head to her breasts. The next thing she knew, he was running his tongue over each nipple and she knew she was lost.

"I have to have you," he said, pressing her so close it was hard to breathe but who needed to breathe, when the sensations came one on top of the other like ripples, building inside as his lips touched her neck and ears and face. She felt herself dampen in anticipation, her lust for him overriding every single thought process but one.

"Make love to me," she murmured pulling him down atop of her.

He kissed her everywhere but her mouth as he undressed her. She'd never made love with him without exchanging a hundred deep, wet kisses that built with the urgency of their passion. But try as she might to trap his face and claim his mouth, he avoided her. At first she thought it was due to that stupid promise and then she caught the glint in his eyes.

He was playing with her.

And she could tell that as soon as he knew she knew, the game stopped. He very slowly lowered his face, millimeter by millimeter, until his lips hovered right above hers, forcing her to reach around his neck and pull him the last inch, crushing their mouths together in a kiss that started in the mouth and instantly traveled everywhere else in her body. His tongue plunged inside her, and to Lara it was as though she absorbed him into herself.

From that moment, everything happened so fast it made her dizzy. Off came the rest of his clothes as they frantically clung to each other, discarding the past as they beat down the door on the present. It was as though the stored-up passion of the past year burst through a dam and swept down a valley, taking them with it, hurtling them against each other in an act as old as time and as new as daybreak.

Until they collapsed against one another, spent, and yet more desirous than ever. If things had been different, Lara would have coaxed him off the floor and between her sheets and done the whole thing again.

So why did this have the feeling of a goodbye?

As though reading her thoughts, he pulled her back into his arms. This time, his kiss was slow and thorough, an almost tender kiss that existed as it was, in the moment it happened.

Afterward, the bittersweet taste of farewell lingered on her lips.

BRADY SPENT the late afternoon returning his father's car to the garage and checking to see if his old man was still out like a light. Surprise, surprise, the house was empty, his dad was gone, no doubt back to River Front Street. For a microsecond, he toyed with the idea of going to fetch him, but in the end, hiked back to his own place and reclaimed his truck. He spent the next couple of hours at the Good Neighbors house, overseeing a few small projects.

It was nearing seven by the time he drove back to the Kirk house. He'd hoped to find Lara packing, but of course she wasn't. The woman was stubborn beyond belief. He had to think of a way to convey the growing conviction in his gut that there was a noose tightening around them.

It was kind of the same feeling he used to get when he was a kid and his parents got into one of their knock-down, drag-out drunken fights. He could remember lying in the top bunk, knowing Garrett was listening to everything, too, trying to figure out how he could make his parents stop, how he could make them see their behavior was hard on his little brother.

And feeling just about as helpless as he did now, when he couldn't find the right words.

After dinner, he moved to the desk, writing down what he knew about the missing Karen Wylie, the wounded Jason Briggs and a wild card named Nicole, a second teenager who wanted to talk to Lara in private.

It all amounted to a lot of nothing and a few maybes. He called Tom and asked if he knew anything about Jason's condition. No change. What must the kid's parents be going through? First, their boy had been part of robbery and car theft that left his best friend dead, followed by months in detention, followed by a gunshot wound less than two days after being released.

He asked Tom if the investigation into the shooting was progressing and got a terse yes. It's police business was the unspoken message.

Brady's gaze wandered to Lara. She sat in the big chair, Nathan on her lap, playing some game with him that involved kissing toes and fingers. She must have felt him looking at her, for she glanced up and met his gaze. Her smoldering eyes made him contemplate getting to his feet.

Myra came into the room, taking care of that urge. "I have the world's worst headache," she told Lara. "Mind if I take something for it and turn in early?"

"Of course not."

She shot Brady a surly parting look that seemed to say, "I know what you're up to, buddy." There was no doubt she sensed the change in the dynamics between

Lara and Brady since they'd argued their way up the stairs and descended smiling at each other.

Lara's voice interrupted his thoughts. "Are you staying here tonight?" she said.

He looked up from his doodling. "I'm staying if you are. I thought that was kind of obvious."

She got to her feet and he saw that Nathan had fallen asleep in her arms. "We're going to bed."

"I'll be along shortly."

She stared at him as she bit her bottom lip. "There's a guest room next to mine," she finally said.

"Good to know. I plan on sleeping with you."

"I—"

"Put Nathan down and come back. I'll wait."

She disappeared up the stairs. Brady tore the doodling paper into little pieces and put them in the trash, then he stood and paced until he heard her footsteps on the stairs.

He turned as she came into the room. "Nothing changed because of this afternoon," he said.

She started picking up baby paraphernalia in what appeared to be a bid not to have to look at him as she said, "I'm so glad to hear you say that. I was worried you might think we're back together."

Her words thundered between them. She glanced up and met his eyes.

He said, "I meant that you and Nathan are still in danger."

"I see," she said softly.

"Tell me what you meant."

She tucked a stuffed bear under one arm as she folded a baby blanket against her chest. Her voice was brisk as she said, "Fabulous sex doesn't change our basic issues."

He took two steps and grabbed her hands, sending

the blanket to the floor again. "Stop talking like a damn counselor."

"That's what I am!"

"Not with me."

"I see. It's okay for your cop persona to exist off-hours but I have to modify what I am?"

What was she talking about? He said, "I do not have a cop persona."

"Give me a break."

"Why did you have sex with me?" he said.

"That's a stupid question."

"Humor me. Never mind, for once, I'll play counselor. For two days you've been trying to get me to sign divorce papers. You've been trying to talk about child support and visitation and joint custody and all the rest of that crap because you couldn't wait to get out of Riverport. And then I finally tell you to go, I'll sign whatever paper you want, just leave so you'll be away from whatever is happening here, and all of a sudden, you won't go."

"That's not how—"

"Yes it is. That's exactly how it happened. You won't go because I want you to go."

"What's that got do with our making love?"

"I don't know," he grumbled. "Maybe you were just trying to distract me."

"Oh, brother." Twisting her hands from his grip, she added, "You better stick with being a cop or building houses or whatever it is you do now, because you're not going to be the next Freud."

"I don't want to be the next Freud. I just want to be the man you can't live without. I just want to be your husband."

She looked straight into his eyes and said, "That's what you had. That's what you sent away when the going got tough."

He had nothing to say to that because her words hit him square where he lived.

"I'm trying to protect you," he said.

"A year ago you tried to protect me from the fallout of the Armstrong shooting. Yesterday you didn't want me to see your family home, you tried to protect me from your past. Now you're trying to protect me from Bill Armstrong's vengeance. You don't know how to include me, Brady. How to include a wife. You love me but you don't know how to be married. I guess after seeing the way you grew up I understand a little—"

"The way I grew up?" he said, because he had to say something, he couldn't just stand there. With a gesture that included the mansion in which they stood, he said, "Look at the way *you* were raised. Do you think you have any more of a grasp on reality than I do?"

"At least my parents allowed *me* to be the child," she said softly.

He stared hard at her, loving her but hating her, too. Hating the emotions she could force on him, hating the power she had to get inside him. Finally, he lowered his gaze and she left the room, climbing the stairs to her childhood bedroom by herself.

He wanted to leave that mausoleum of a house in the worst way possible. He opened the front door and looked out onto the dark, empty street. How could he leave his family unprotected? But how could he stand to sit still? He dug a blanket out of the hall closet and emptied his pockets, then stared at the chair.

A moment later, he was locking the front door

behind him. Hands shoved in pockets, he took off down the dark sidewalk, forcing himself to turn at the corner and make a circle and then a larger one and another, the Kirk house always the hub even when he went blocks without actually seeing it. After more than an hour, he finally started back to the house.

No amount of walking would erase the sound of Lara's voice in his head: *At least my parents allowed me to be the child.*

It had been a ridiculous thing for her to say. He'd been a child....

No, he hadn't.

That's why her words stung. She was right and he knew it. What he didn't know was how to fix it.

He approached the big house with his head down, determined to stand guard outside, swearing to himself he would never go inside the place again. He glanced up as he stopped on the porch. His mouth went dry.

An orange glow in the sitting-room window danced and flickered. Fire!

He fumbled in his pocket for his keys, banging on the door and yelling as he did so. He finally found the keys and shoved the right one into the lock, pushed open the door and stepped into the foyer, looking toward the sitting room.

Flames leaped up the draperies, traveling toward him even as he watched, using the carpets for fuel. He reached for the phone on the small table by the grandfather clock and found the line dead. Grabbing from the floor the baby blanket Lara had dropped an hour or so before, he covered his nose and mouth and took off up the stairs, taking them two at a time.

The second floor was smokier than the first and he coughed as he ran down the hall to Lara's room, surprised to find the end of the hall a wall of fire.

Her door was closed and locked. He raised a leg and kicked the door in, doing his best to shut it afterward, but it was no use, he'd shattered the frame. Lara sat up upon his entry. She'd fallen asleep with the bedside lamp on and it miraculously still worked. Her expression went from surprised to horrified with her first conscious breath of smoke-laden air.

She immediately started coughing and he pulled her from the bed. "Get some shoes on. Hurry," he said as he ran to the crib where he picked up Nathan. Ignoring the baby's startled cries, Brady wrapped him in layers of baby sheets and blankets, tucking up loose ends as fast as he could. Lara was at his side by then, wearing nothing but a T-shirt, underpants and slippers. He handed Nathan to her then guided her back across the room to the door.

The flames had traveled down the hall, again fueled by expensive carpets laid over hardwood floors. "Fire in the kitchen must be coming up the old dumbwaiter," Lara said.

"We'll make a run for the stairs," Brady said, until he remembered the fire in the sitting room downstairs and wondered if those flames had managed to climb the stairs yet. If they had, would he be leading his family into an inferno?

"The solarium roof," Lara said, turning and running back to her window. He took a moment to push a dresser in front of the broken door, hoping to stop the flames for as long as possible. Both Lara and Nathan were coughing by the time he got to the window.

It was the old-fashioned double-hung kind and she was struggling with one arm to get the bottom panel raised. "Keep the baby down near the floor, honey, under the smoke," he said, and she dropped immediately. He worked on the window until he got it far enough open to kick out the screen. The fire would seek this new outlet soon, he could already see flames licking the edge of the door.

Lara pulled on his jeans and he knelt, coughing into the baby blanket he'd somehow managed to keep hold of. "The solarium juts out from the back of the house," she said. "It's about a ten-foot drop to the roof."

"You go first. I'll drop Nathan to you."

"No, you go—"

He grabbed her by the arm, took Nathan, laid him on the floor by their feet and lifted her to the window. "Hurry," he said.

Her gaze slid from the door to his eyes. "I love you," she said.

"I love you, too. Now, climb out. Perch on the sill, take my hands, I'll lower you as far as I can, then you'll have to drop."

She immediately climbed into the window and leveraged herself outside. He gripped her hands and she used her feet to rappel against the outside wall until his arms were stretched tight, her weight dragging him farther out the window.

"Let go," she called, and he dropped her. He heard a thud a second later. She yelled she was okay.

The lamp snapped off as electricity to the house was lost. Brady picked up Nathan and tightened the swaddling around his struggling body, the baby's cries bruising his heart. Over and over, Brady prayed that his son would make it through this night, and he kissed the tear-stained cheeks.

The flaw in their plan showed itself when Brady held Nathan outside the window and found he couldn't really see Lara's exact location. How could he drop his son if he couldn't see?

And then, like a miracle, a brief flash of light from the ground scanned the side of the house and he caught a glimpse of Lara standing right beneath his position. A second later the light flickered off, but now Brady knew where Lara was.

"Here he comes," he called, and dropped his son.

A second later, broken words floated up to him, reaching his ears like music. "I…I caught…him." And this was followed by some very healthy baby bellows.

He was on the verge of making the jump himself when movement in the yard caught his attention. A man ran beneath the weak light affixed to the end of the small dock out by the river. The dock light was apparently on its own circuit. The man hurried along the dock and disappeared over the side. A second later, a boat detached itself and was lost on the dark water.

"Brady!" Lara screamed.

"I'm coming."

"What about Myra?"

He jumped, landing on his feet and hands, his bad knee buckling under him, pitching him forward. He caught himself a few inches from the edge of the roof.

"What about Myra?" Lara said again, grabbing his arm, her voice barely audible over the sound of the fire and her son's wailing.

"I'll go get her. Where exactly is her room?"

"On the other side of the kitchen."

They used the wisteria trellis nailed against the solarium wall to get to the ground, both of them pausing for a second to look at the house, both of them stunned with how far the fire had spread. It appeared to have started in three or four places at once.

He took Lara's arm and they ran around the solarium to the kitchen where flames glowed through the windows.

"Myra's room is on the other side," Lara said.

"Go to a neighbor's house. Make sure the fire department's been called. I'll get her out."

"You shouldn't go back in—"

"Go," he urged, pushing her away.

She ran from him as he stuck the baby blanket in a birdbath and used the kettle barbecue like a battering ram to break the window into the laundry that adjoined the kitchen.

The wet blanket went around his shoulders, over his head. The laundry was filled with smoke. The kitchen fire wasn't as bad as it had seemed from the outside, and he was able to dash through.

A narrow door on the far side of the counter, back in an alcove he'd never noticed before, had to be Myra's door. There were flames in front of the door. He grabbed a kitchen chair and banged it against the door, hoping the noise would wake the woman. Using his wet blanket, he grabbed the knob and wrenched the door open, running into a room so filled with smoke it was hard to take a breath.

He'd have one chance at this, he knew. If she'd staggered out of bed and fallen in a corner, he'd never find her in time. He dashed to the bed and threw back the covers.

Light from the fire showed him the shape of a woman in the bed. He grabbed her shoulders, but she didn't stir. He didn't dare take time to assess her condition, and leaning down, lifted her over his shoulder in a fireman's hold. He ran back the way he'd come, through the flames and the smoke, through the kitchen into the laundry room and out the backdoor.

He heard sirens in the distance. Man, he loved that sound.

He got Myra as far away from the house as he could, out near the flowers under the trees, and lowered her to the grass. She looked at him with dazed eyes, and then she, too, began coughing.

He waited until she caught her breath and checked her pulse. Her color was returning to normal.

"Where am I?" she said as she seemed to see him for the first time. She sputtered, "Who are—oh my goodness, is that you, Brady? What happened?"

Brady stepped aside so she could see past him to the now towering inferno.

"Lara and the baby—"

"They're safe. I want to go find them. Will you be okay?"

"Yes."

He ran toward the house until he saw a figure jog around the corner. Lara's voice screamed, "Brady! Brady!"

He yelled as he moved toward her. "Get away from there!" He was afraid she'd be cut if the windows blew.

She turned in his direction. He could see the outline of her slender body, thanks to the burning house behind her, but he couldn't see her face. She started running toward him, covering the distance in a very short time, long bare legs flashing in the light of the blaze.

He caught her in his arms.

THE FIREFIGHTERS COULDN'T stop talking about the chances of two house fires in two days, even if they were in separate towns and nineteen miles apart. What were the chances?

Pretty good, Brady thought. If an arsonist wanted to get rid of two people in two different places, two fires might just do the job.

"I have to leave for a while," he told Lara.

She'd reclaimed Nathan from the neighbor she'd left him with while she came to look for Brady and was now standing near the ambulance crew and Myra.

"Do you have to?"

"Yes."

"Myra's sister offered to take us all in for the night. She's on her way over." She looked down at herself and added, her voice kind of awestruck, "I don't have any clothes."

One of the firefighters had given her a blue blanket that she had draped over her scantily clad body and over Nathan, too. The little guy had fallen asleep again.

Brady cupped the back of Lara's head and kissed her forehead, his heart aching with the things he wanted to say to her. "I'll be back soon."

"The police—"

"That's why I have to get out of here right now, before they start asking questions."

She looked up at him, her eyes watering still from the smoke. "You know who did this, don't you?"

"Yes."

"Was it Armstrong?"

"Yes. I saw him out by the dock. He left in a boat."

"Why don't you wait until Tom—"

"No," Brady said. "Not this time."

"Take your gun," she said.

Chapter Eleven

Brady didn't need a gun. He was mad enough to take Bill Armstrong apart with his bare hands. A gun would just get in the way.

Too late he realized his truck keys were in the burned-up house along with his cell phone and wallet. He ran the mile to his place in record time. He kept the Harley key hidden on the bike and within seconds of hitting his parking lot, roared off into the night without a helmet, as that was locked inside his apartment.

All the lights were on at the Armstrong house despite the fact it was two-thirty in the morning. Brady left the Harley a couple doors down. No need to announce his arrival.

He kept to the shadows as he moved quickly through the yard. He was sure Tom or another Riverport cop would arrive any minute and he wanted a few moments alone with Armstrong before that happened.

In the end, he was left with a decision: knock on the door or break it down. One or the other. If he barged in, he was likely to be blown away by a shotgun wielded either by a crazy Bill Armstrong or his terrified wife. No jury in the world would blame either one of them.

He knocked.

The door opened at once. His heart lurched in anticipation, but it was Sandra who peered through the crack at him, not Bill.

"What's happened?" she said, her hand bunching her robe up near her throat, her knuckles shiny white.

"Do you know where your husband is, Mrs. Armstrong?"

She stared at him so long he wasn't sure she was going to answer. She finally said, "He's gone." As if to prove he wasn't there, she opened the door wider and stepped aside.

He entered the house warily, though he had a hard time believing Sandra Armstrong would purposefully set him up for murder.

The room was lit to the point of glaring brightness, obliterating any dark corners, revealing every secret. Immaculately kept to the point of starkness, the only ornaments, and there were literally dozens of them, were framed pictures of two good-looking brunette kids, one girl and one boy, no more than a year or so apart in age. The pictures were a chronicle of their lives, starting with a small toddler sitting by a baby lying on a blanket, up to the same children as teenagers dressed for a dance or a party, standing side by side, looking kind of impatient at having to pose and yet vibrant and alive.

He was standing in the middle of a shrine dedicated to the memory of Bill and Sandra Armstrong's children, one dead by her own hand, the other gunned down by Brady Skye.

"What happened to you?" Sandra Armstrong gasped. He caught his reflection on the blank television screen. Six-foot-one-inch of soot-covered male who looked angry and crushed at the same time.

"Someone set my wife's mother's house on fire tonight, Mrs. Armstrong."

She clutched her robe up high, under her chin again. Her pale skin seemed to drain of even more color. Her eyes went wide with shock and pain and he once again wished he was anywhere but standing in front of her.

What would learning of her husband's actions of the last few days do to her? What would happen to her if Lara's theory was right and she discovered her husband had molested their daughter and her girlfriends?

"I need to talk to Bill," he said.

"He didn't do it," she protested. "He wouldn't—"

"He was there, Mrs. Armstrong. I saw him."

She staggered and he grabbed her elbows, guiding her to a chair. She sat down stiffly. He perched on the edge of another chair to face her eye to eye.

"I can understand why you and your husband hate me," he said. "I don't blame you. But your husband either tried to kill my family tonight or he knows who did. I have to talk to him."

She stared at him for another of those interminable minutes before she finally muttered, "He came home late. He'd been drinking. He was talking to himself. I tried to get him to go to bed but he wouldn't do it. Instead he went out to the garage and banged around out there for a long time. I finally went to see what he was doing. He was…he was loading the truck."

"Loading the truck?"

"I thought maybe he was going to go camping or something. I thought it might be a good idea if he left town for a few days and stopped obsessing about your son. He loaded his skiff in the back. Fishing, I thought.

The outboard motor came next and then two or three fuel cans—"

He stopped her. "Fuel cans? Why so many?"

This time her stare challenged him to connect the dots.

"And then he left," she mumbled.

"And you haven't seen him since then?"

Another pause as she searched his eyes. "He came back less than an hour ago. He smelled like, like smoke."

"You have to tell me where he is now, Mrs. Armstrong. He has to be stopped."

"He left again," she said. "He didn't tell me where he was going or when he was coming back."

There wasn't a doubt in Brady's mind Armstrong had shined that light on the burning house, which meant he knew Lara, at least, had escaped. He got to his feet in a hurry. He had to get back to Lara and Nathan.

Sandra Armstrong caught his arm at the door. Her wide eyes seemed to swallow him. "Please," she said. "Please, you have to help Bill."

"I'll try," he said, anxious to get going.

But it was obvious there was something else she needed to say and he made himself stand there for the few seconds it took her to add, "He took a rifle with him."

TOM WAS WALKING UP the sidewalk as Brady left the Armstrong house.

"Lara wouldn't tell me where you went, but I figured it was over here," he said, hitching his hands on his belt. "You left the scene of a crime."

"I have to go," he said, not stopping to talk.

Tom called, "Wait a second."

Brady paused and looked back over his shoulder.

"I'm in a hurry. Lara took Nathan over to the house-keeper's sister's house. I have to get over there."

"The fire investigator will be here in a few hours," Tom interrupted. "The place reeks of gasoline fumes. There were several fires started. Do you have any reason to suspect Bill Armstrong?" He nodded toward the house. "Is he in there?"

"No," Brady said, but knew he had to explain. He hurriedly told Tom what he'd seen that night and the conversation he'd just had with Sandra Armstrong.

Tom shook his head. "Dixon isn't going to like you coming over here—"

"I don't care what Dixon does or doesn't like," Brady said. "He's not my boss, he's yours."

"And you're my partner."

"I *was* your partner."

"I'm just telling you to stay out of my way. Is that too much to ask?"

Brady leveled a stare at his ex-partner. "Bill Armstrong tried to kill my wife and son tonight. Now he's out there somewhere with a gun. So the answer to your question is yes. Asking me to leave everything to you is asking too much." And with that he took off down the sidewalk to reclaim the Harley.

Once on his bike, he realized he had no idea where Myra's sister lived or even what her name was. He returned to the Kirk house where he found firefighters putting out the last of the blaze. Tom's new partner, the Hastings kid Brady had first met the night Lara's car went into the river, was attempting to keep the small crowd of onlookers—mostly neighbors, it seemed—at a safe distance. Brady recognized the local newspaper reporter and gave him a wide berth.

What would Lara's mother think of him now that he'd been indirectly responsible for the destruction of her home? He hoped she kept up her insurance payments.

One of the firefighters was an old friend and called out to Brady. He passed along a message from Lara, giving him Myra's sister's address. Brady rode the Harley to the woman's house, which turned out to be less than a mile from his place, and spent hours standing guard, filthy and tired but strangely wide awake. When Bill Armstrong failed to appear by daybreak, Brady went back to his apartment, roused the manager for a spare key and took a shower.

He guessed it was up to the police to find Armstrong. His job was to keep Lara and Nathan safe.

LARA HAPPILY TOOK OFF the robe Myra's sister, Gretchen, had loaned her and changed into the sweatpants and T-shirt Brady had brought her from his apartment. The clothes were a little big, but they smelled like him and that was comforting.

She exited the bathroom to find Brady sitting on the guest bed next to Nathan, who wore diapers fashioned from kitchen towels and nothing else. The baby was clean and pink again, declared healthy by the EMTs. And he was safe, at least for the moment.

"I need to do some shopping," Lara said, leaning over to kiss Nathan's bare tummy.

Brady pulled her onto his lap and nuzzled her neck. She closed her eyes for a second and relaxed in his arms. She owed him her life and that of her son. He'd even risked himself to save Myra.

But in the end, it didn't change the basic facts of their differences.

He finally said, "You don't have credit cards or cash. I'll go with you."

"I'll pay you back—"

He tightened his grip around her waist and interrupted her. "I want you to know I won't ask you to leave Riverport again. You were right. Until Armstrong is behind bars, you and Nathan belong right here. We'll talk about what comes next later. I'll stop pressuring you."

She drew back a few inches and narrowed her eyes. "Who the heck are you and what have you done with Brady Skye?"

He laughed at her lame joke and she took a deep breath.

"I know we're lucky to be alive," she said. "I'm thankful for that, I really am. But when I think of my mother's house I just want to cry. How am I ever going to explain all this to her?"

"Maybe if you let her hold Nathan as you tell her, she'll keep her priorities straight."

"I know that. But her whole life went up in flames. My childhood, too. That counts for something."

He opened his mouth to answer, but the words died on his lips. He'd been about to say, *Be grateful you had a childhood to lose.*

He wouldn't say it. He couldn't. Besides, she didn't need an argument, she was just telling him that she'd lost something important.

"She'll understand," he said, hoping it was the truth. "If she's honest, she'll realize her dislike of fire alarms could have resulted in your deaths."

"I hope that decision doesn't void her policy." With a sigh, she added, "I guess there's nothing I can do about any of it now."

"I guess not."

MOST OF THE DAY was taken up with replacing the clothing and accessories lost in the fire and calling credit-card companies and anyone else they could think of who needed to know their identification had been destroyed.

After shopping, they spoke to countless officials, including Chief Dixon, who kept staring at Nathan whom Brady held. *Let him say one word about "Another Skye," and I'll punch him into next week,* Brady thought, but Dixon reserved his comments for the fire. Tom had been right. Dixon was irked that Brady had gone to Armstrong's house after they escaped the blaze and told him so. Brady ignored him.

The truth was, the whole department knew Brady had placed Bill Armstrong at the scene. It was also common knowledge Armstrong was coming unglued. The fact he was now running around town with a gun had everyone on edge.

"Chief Dixon said they think it was Bill who shot Jason. He said they've gone to his house and looked for guns."

Brady imagined how that intrusion must have felt to Sandra Armstrong. If he could find Bill, maybe he would ease some of her pain. He owed her that much. Lara glanced at her new watch and added, "It's getting late. Let's take Nathan back to Myra and go talk to Nicole."

"Do you think she and Gretchen can keep Nathan safe?"

"Are you kidding? Gretchen is armed to the teeth. She stayed up all last night patrolling the house while Myra, Nathan and I slept."

"I didn't see her," Brady said skeptically, "and I was outside."

"Maybe you didn't see her, honey, but she saw you."

AFTER THE FLOOD a few years earlier, the city of Riverport had applied for and received a grant from the state to rebuild their city park. Walkways and fences had been constructed almost immediately, but it had taken until the year before for the new playground to take shape. Everyone agreed it had been worth waiting for, however, as it was a modern structure that combined slides, rock-wall climbers, sliding poles and bridges within the illusion of a ship.

They parked with a few other cars and walked across the grass where two kids braved the ninety-degree heat to play on the adjoining swings. A lone adult-size figure stood to the side, yelling at one of the children to stop swinging the other so high. The one close to orbit screamed at the top of his lungs.

Lara barely recognized Nicole from the few times she'd seen her at the teen center in the company of her friends. Her long, shiny black hair was short now, spiky, with bright pink and blue tips. Her hair wasn't the only thing that had changed. The kid had grown three inches and developed a curvy figure. She wore a gauzy navy blouse emblazoned with golden swirls, cutoffs and strappy sandals.

"Nicole?" Lara said when they were a few feet away.

The girl turned. She smiled when she saw Lara, though the smile faltered as they got closer and she seemed to realize the tall man trailing Lara was actually with her.

"This is my friend Brady," Lara said. She could almost feel Brady wince when she called him her friend.

"I know who he is," Nicole said. "I saw his picture in the paper. He killed Sara's little brother."

Lara didn't dare turn around and look at Brady whose whole body she imagined had tensed. Instead, she jumped into the ensuing silence with, "Brady is more than a friend, he's also an ex-cop, as you seem to know. Let's sit down, okay?"

The girl said, "I won't talk in front of him."

Brady took a look around the park as though searching for snipers. With a start, Lara realized that's exactly what he was doing. Looking for Bill Armstrong. And that's why they'd taken the circuitous route to the park. He'd been checking for a tail. He said, "I'm going to go sit right over there and check out the water fountain, Lara. Call if you need me."

Lara and Nicole both watched Brady walk across the playground. Nicole said, "He should be in jail."

Lara motioned at the bench and they sat down. Staring at the kids who were now scooting up and down the ladders and slides, she said, "Brady Skye is a very decent, honorable man who pays every day of his life for being forced to shoot Sara's brother. But right now, we're both trying to figure out what Jason Briggs wanted to tell me. Do you know?"

Nicole answered the question with one of her own. "I heard about the fire at the Kirk mansion. Do they know who did it?"

"We think the same man who started the fire has been hanging around a lot, making threats."

Shouting erupted from the play equipment. Nicole stood abruptly, took a few steps forward and said, "Sammy, you stop that or I'll tell your mother."

Sammy was tugging the other kid down the slide by

his hair. Both the children started laughing as they slapped at each other. They ignored Nicole.

Nicole sat down again and faced Lara, looking younger than before. "I'm never having kids. Never."

Lara said, "You said you wanted to talk to me about Karen Wylie."

"She called me. You know, the day you guys came into the pharmacy and talked to her. She called me after you left. You spooked her. She told me she was going to go away with her boyfriend, that they were going to get married. She said it was his idea."

"Her boyfriend?" No one had mentioned a boyfriend though they all now knew she'd met up with a man in Scottsdell.

"But she was lying," Nicole added.

"How do you know?"

"Because the man she thought was her boyfriend is nobody's boyfriend," she said, her voice suddenly softer. "That's not how he…operates."

"And how do you know this?"

She glanced quickly at Lara and away again. "I just do. He and I…it doesn't matter. Anyway, he's still in town."

Nicole looked around as she spoke, as though watching for someone. Her nerves got to Lara, who lowered her voice, too. "Who is this man?"

Nicole stared at the kids. They were at each other again. "I can't tell you."

"Nicole—"

"I can't. I won't."

"Then why did you want to talk to me?"

She shrugged one thin shoulder. "I kind of like Mrs. Wylie. I know she's worried. I'm just telling you that Karen didn't run away with a boyfriend, that's all."

"Then why did she go?"

"Because she's stupid about guys. She thinks she's going to be a movie star. The girl is stupid." Nicole stared into the distance and then added, "And *he's* mean."

"This man?"

"Yes."

"In what way?"

She shook her head so hard the colored tips looked like confetti. "I'm not going to say any more."

"You're afraid of him."

Nicole nodded. "He's got a lot of power."

"I have to have a name. The police will want to talk to you."

She stood abruptly, ready to bolt.

"Listen," Lara said, standing beside her. "I know you girls spent a lot of time at the Armstrong house when Sara was still alive. I know he befriended you. Is it Bill Armstrong?"

Nicole bit her lip.

"I can help if you'll confide in me. There are laws against hurting people."

Nicole met Lara's gaze and laughed.

Brady strode across the playground. "Everything okay?"

"I don't know," Lara said, and paraphrased what Nicole had told her. Nicole wouldn't meet Brady's gaze.

"Call your mother," he urged. "Get her to come over here—"

"I can't," Nicole said. "This is the boys' afternoon to be at the park. I have to watch them."

"Bill Armstrong is running around with a gun,"

Brady said. "Take the boys back to their parents' house and stay there until your own mother comes home."

A few minutes later, Nicole piled the kids into her tiny blue car and drove off. A sticker on the rear window read, Riverport High School honor student.

Lara said, "I blew that. She tried to reach out and I blew it."

Brady's voice sounded speculative as he said, "I keep thinking I've seen her before."

"Has she ever been in trouble with the cops?"

"I don't know."

"Maybe—"

Both Lara and Brady had replaced their phones earlier in the day and now Brady's rang, interrupting Lara. He answered it quickly, surprised to hear Myra's voice, though her attitude toward him had undergone a decided thaw since he'd rescued her from the fire.

"The hospital is trying to get hold of Lara," Myra said. "They called the police who called Gretchen who called me, but I can't find the phone number Lara gave me, but I could find yours."

Lara called the hospital and after identifying herself, listened with growing attention. "I'll be right there," she said at last and, clicking off the phone, touched Brady's arm. "Jason Briggs is conscious and he's asking for me."

THEY ARRIVED at the hospital to find a guard on Jason's door. Chief Dixon was also standing close by and he barred Brady's admittance. "The kid wants to talk to Ms. Kirk," Dixon said. "He didn't say nothing about you."

"Have you found Bill Armstrong yet?" Brady

asked in a low voice Lara recognized as his voice of massive control.

"No," Dixon said. "But we will."

Lara said, "How long has Jason been conscious?"

"Not long. We've had a guard on his door since the first night. Only his doctors and parents have been allowed in. His parents are on their way over, so if I were you, I'd get in there. I'm sending in a police officer, too, to take notes of what he says. The doctors say you can have five minutes, no more."

Leaving the two men to glare at one another, Lara entered the room quietly. Jason Briggs, last seen unconscious lying on the grass, didn't look a lot better lying in the hospital bed. Almost as pale as his sheets, his black hair stark against his skin, hospital apparatus blipped and beeped all around him.

A nurse stepped to one side to allow Lara to lean close. Lara whispered, "Jason?"

The boy's eyes fluttered open as though he'd been waiting for her. His breathing sounded labored.

"Hey, Jason," Lara said. He looked so young and vulnerable, and for a second, she flashed on the moment she'd lost hold of him in the car as it filled with water, the frantic grabbing for his hair to pull him back to the surface…

"Ms. Kirk," Jason whispered.

"I'm here."

His eyes closed and she felt a stab of disappointment. She glanced at the police officer, who shrugged. As she started to straighten, Jason's eyes opened again. "Ms. Kirk?"

She put her hand on his shoulder. "Yes, Jason, I'm still here."

"It was…fossil…blue," Jason said. "Billy…"

Fossil? What did that mean?

"The Colt…"

Billy, blue fossils, colt—the memory came back with a flash. Billy and Jason at the teen center, an overheard conversation about an old Colt revolver…

Aware the officer was writing down everything Billy said, Lara's heart all but stopped beating as she murmured, "Are you talking about a gun, Jason? Did Billy Armstrong have a gun the night he was shot?"

"His grandpa's," Jason whispered.

Lara felt like smacking herself. The knowledge of the gun had been niggling at her memory since she returned to Riverport and talked to Brady that first afternoon. "I understand," she said, aching to tell Brady. She waited patiently as Jason's eyes drifted shut, but once again, when she moved, he rallied. "Karen?"

"Karen? You mean Karen Wylie?"

Jason nodded. "Talk…to…her."

"I'm sorry," Lara said softly. "She's…well, out of town."

He grew restless as he reached up and grabbed Lara's wrist. His grip was amazingly strong. "No," he said.

Karen's name was all Jason had managed to say before someone shot him. She'd been on his mind since he got out of juvie. Lara said, "What is it about Karen?"

His hand slid from her wrist. "Naked," he said, licking dry lips. His voice was so soft both Lara and the attending officer leaned in closer to hear.

"Karen was naked?"

He nodded again.

"I don't understand—"

He whispered, "Bad pictures."

He was fading in and out. The nurse who had been standing cleared her throat. Lara said, "Jason, one more thing. Did Billy's father ever—"

"Ms. Kirk," Chief Dixon said sternly from the doorway.

"I'm coming," she told him. The officer stopped writing and took a step toward the door.

Jason said, "Mr. Armstr—"

"Ms. Kirk?"

Lara glanced up at Dixon, annoyed beyond endurance. "Please, just give me a moment!" She looked back down at Jason, but his eyes had shut again, and this time when she gently touched his shoulder there was no response.

The nurse examined him quickly. "He's just asleep," she said after a moment. "You'd better go now."

Lara looked around at the officer who had been taking notes. "Did you hear what he said about the gun?"

He grinned. "Every word."

Lara walked past Dixon, out into the hall, walked right up to Brady and took his hands.

"Billy Armstrong had a gun the night he died," she said. "He was carrying an old Colt with blue-fossil grips. I actually remember hearing the boys talk about it a week or so before the shooting. They were practically drooling. I think Billy stole it from his grandmother's house. I doubt she ever knew it was gone."

"Then he wasn't unarmed?" Brady said softly.

"No."

"I did see him pull a gun?" he said, his voice reflecting the growing wonder of this discovery.

"You must have, because a gun like that never showed up in the investigation, did it?"

"No, and they tore the place apart. The car, too."

"The gun fell into the river."

His eyes glistened as he put his arms around her, lifted her off her feet and buried his head against her neck.

Chapter Twelve

"Jason also tried to say something about Billy's father," Lara said as they drove back to Myra's house. "That damn Chief Dixon interrupted and Jason fell asleep before he could finish his thought."

"Dixon has impeccably bad timing," Brady said. They were driving his truck. As disappointing as it was that Lara hadn't heard what the boy had to say about Bill Armstrong, Brady was still riding high on the euphoria of knowing Billy had had a gun.

He hadn't shot an unarmed kid. He felt twenty years younger, twenty pounds lighter, the day appeared twenty times brighter. "What do you think he was trying to say about Karen?"

"The naked-picture thing? I have no idea."

"We'll ask Armstrong, if we ever find him."

There were two police units parked in front of Gretchen's house. Tom James and Chief Dixon stood outside talking to Myra. The housekeeper looked up as Brady slowed the truck. She'd been crying.

"Something's wrong," Lara said, fumbling with the door handle. Brady was outside and around to her side in a flash. Together they ran across the grass.

In that ten seconds, Brady died a thousand deaths. He shouldn't have left Nathan unguarded. He should have stayed with the baby instead of going with Lara to the hospital. He should have insisted they all stay together.

Myra burst into new tears when she saw Lara but it was Brady to whom she turned, almost collapsing in his arms. "He tried to take the little dear," she cried.

Lara's gasp seemed to suck in a gallon of air. Brady immediately put an arm around her.

"He tried? Who tried?"

"Armstrong," Tom said.

Myra's watery eyes searched Lara's face as she added, "I only left him on the porch alone for a moment, I swear. The breeze comes through that way and it's so much cooler. He was asleep in his new car seat. I cracked the door and went back inside for iced tea. I shouldn't have left him, this is all my fault. I just went away for a moment. When I came back, there was Bill Armstrong, big as you please, walking out the door with the baby still in his car seat."

Lara grabbed Myra's arm. "But he didn't actually hurt Nathan, right? Nathan is okay, isn't he?"

"I threw my iced tea at Bill! He dropped the seat—"

Lara's hands flew to her mouth.

"It didn't hurt the baby, the little lamb never even woke up! He's inside with Gretchen, right as rain."

Lara took off at a run toward the house, Myra on her heels.

Tom cleared his throat and looked at Brady. "Apparently, the housekeeper's scream alerted the other lady, who attacked Armstrong with a dust mop. He ran off after that and they called us."

Dixon added, "We've got everyone and their brother looking for him. He can't have gone far."

Brady clenched his jaw. He'd been trying for days to get the department to take the threat of Armstrong seriously and now they were stuck playing catch-up. Icy-hot fury flamed in his gut, but he swallowed hard and directed his anger where it belonged—at Bill Armstrong. The man was out of control, capable of anything.

Not with my son...

"The lab boys will be here any minute," Dixon said, sparing Brady an uneasy half glance. "I'll get a patrol car out here, too, until we find Armstrong. Tom, I want you on the street with the others."

Tom touched his gun, his eyes blazing as he looked at Brady. "You stay here with Lara, buddy, she needs you. I'll find the bastard."

"That's right," Dixon said. "This is a job for professionals."

Tom strode off to his car. Dixon produced a pack from his pocket and tapped out a cigarette. He looked up at Brady as he lit it and said, "I know the Briggs kid said the Armstrong boy had a gun."

"Yeah," Brady said.

Putting the cigarette to his lips, he inhaled deeply. "It doesn't change a thing," he said as he exhaled a cloud of smoke. "We're better off without you."

Brady met Dixon's gaze and said, "At least I don't go around making passes at little girls."

Dixon snatched the cigarette from his lips, threw it to the sidewalk and stomped it out. "Where did you—"

"Hear about your first marriage? Hear why my mother divorced you?"

Dixon finally sputtered, "The kid I supposedly propositioned was a few months shy of seventeen. She did the propositioning, by the way. I married her after the divorce."

"I heard she was thirteen."

"Your father won Theresa and then he destroyed her. I guess he showed me."

Brady didn't blink.

Dixon cast him one more baleful glance before turning on his heels. Brady jogged to the house as the chief drove off. Lara, holding Nathan, looked up at him and smiled as he opened the door. Brady was across the room in two steps, gathering his wife and son in a huge embrace.

They were his salvation. They were the reason he wouldn't turn out like his father or Chief Dixon.

There was a loud knock on the door. Gretchen appeared from the kitchen and admitted the lab guys. Casting Lara and Brady an apologetic smile, she disappeared into the house to show them the way to the porch, which they would process.

As soon as the swinging door closed behind them, Brady leaned down and claimed Lara's lips. He kissed her with relief, joy, fear, anger—it was all part and parcel of being alive. He wanted her in the worst way possible, not for an hour or a few stolen moments. He wanted her forever. And he wanted her to want him.

"I should have left when you asked me to," she said, searching his face. "Now I'm afraid to go. He's out there. I can feel his eyes on the back of my neck. I can feel his hatred. He'll never quit until he's hurt Nathan."

"I won't let that happen," Brady said. "It's gone on far too long as it is. I'll take care of it."

"But Tom—"

The memory of Tom's fingers dancing near his gun as he vowed to find Bill Armstrong surfaced in Brady's mind. He said, "If Tom finds Armstrong first he's likely to do something impulsive. I've got to stop him before he sabotages himself. Chief Dixon said he'd send a patrol car over. As soon as it comes, I'm going to go find Armstrong and put an end to this."

She stared at him a long moment before finally nodding. "Okay."

He caught her hand and held it against his chest. "I'm so sorry I wasn't vigilant enough."

"Oh, Brady, listen to us," she said. "I'm to blame, you're to blame. What difference does it make?"

It made a lot of difference to Brady. He kissed her again. "I'm crazy in love with you," he whispered against her lips. "I've never loved another woman. I never will." It was on the tip of his tongue to promise to become the man she wanted, open and happy-go-lucky and willing to examine every dark corner of his subconscious. But the words wouldn't come.

As he kissed Nathan's forehead, she whispered, "Be careful."

A PATROL OFFICER Brady didn't recognize arrived a few minutes later and Brady left. He drove to his apartment and let himself in with his new house key. It took him a couple of minutes to find his backup key for the dresser drawer, but once he did, he reached for the Glock without hesitation.

He strapped on his holster and despite everything, hoped he'd find a way through the ensuing hours to bring in Armstrong without drawing the gun.

As he got into his truck again, he tried to clear his

head and organize his thoughts. Bill Armstrong was coming apart. He was acting on impulse, striking out. Where would he go between strikes? Where would he feel safe?

Okay, maybe not safe. Where would he feel connected, where would he feel some kind of comfort? Somewhere apart from his wife's consuming grief. Someplace private and meaningful.

At the graveyard where his two kids had been buried side by side?

Think, Brady. Where would you go if you were Bill Armstrong? What if the need for revenge ate up every available brain synapse? What if the past felt twice as real as the present, the past was all you had left besides hate? Where would you go to think up your next idea to hurt the man who killed your son?

And then he knew.

HE DROVE to the old Evergreen Timber-mill site, his heartbeat accelerating when he found the chain and lock securing the repaired gate had been sawed apart and looped through the fence again so it would appear linked to all but a careful observer.

He left the truck parked down the block and let himself in through the gate. The afternoon had faded to evening, the hot, oppressive air weighed down on him as he walked, memories of a year ago dogged his heels.

He reached the place where Jason had wrecked the car and the two boys had sprung from it like rats leaving a downed ship. Armstrong's truck was parked almost in the same spot, the back empty now.

And parked beside it, a police unit. Tom's car.

He should have known Tom would have reached the same conclusion he had. He made a quick examination of both vehicles then took off to the right, veering toward the river, following the invisible path he'd traveled a year before.

He stopped when he got close to the spot Billy Armstrong's life had ended. A feeling of déjà vu struck as he heard an Armstrong voice raised in anger, but this time it belonged to the father instead of the son. It came from behind a nearby stack of abandoned railroad ties.

He moved in that direction, balancing stealth with the burning need to see what was going on. Was Tom with Armstrong? He strained for the sound of another voice, but Armstrong's ramblings obliterated everything, even the sound of the river rushing by.

Armstrong's words grew more distinctive. "Voices, voices," he cried. "Day and night, voices, bad voices telling me what to do, a son for a son, retribution will be mine!"

The words froze Brady's heart, but not his step. Crazy people did crazy things. Where was Tom? Had Armstrong already turned the tables on him? Was Tom still alive?

Moving a few steps, Brady peered carefully around the pile and saw Armstrong standing near the edge of the wharf. The man was as gray as the river at twilight. Even his sandy hair and beard had faded, though that was no doubt a trick of light.

Armstrong began pacing back and forth near the edge, mumbling one moment, shouting another, stabbing at thin air. He didn't appear to be armed, though a rifle lay a few feet away.

Brady couldn't see Tom, but the sound of his friend's

voice finally filled a lull in Armstrong's ramblings. "You've done too many evil things, you've caused too much pain," Tom said.

Brady took a deep breath. Tom was still alive.

"I know, it's true," Armstrong said, all but crying now. Brady shifted his position and managed to see Tom through a crack in the railroad ties. He stood a good twenty yards away, florid face flushed a shade darker than usual. He stood with his feet planted out to either side, arm extended, gun in hand, pointed at Armstrong.

Worse, the tension that boiled in Tom's body seemed to cause a disturbance in the air around him. He looked like a cartoon bomb, fuse lit, ready to explode.

Undoubtedly, Tom had called in his position and his sighting of Armstrong's truck, which meant the police would arrive within minutes. Should Brady stand by and wait or should he try to defuse the situation himself?

Armstrong began shouting again, and this time Tom's voice was raised, too. Brady made the only decision that made sense to him. He slowly stepped around the ties, the Glock in its holster, his hands spread out to the sides.

Both of the other men immediately looked at him.

Armstrong took a step in his direction. He said, "Your son. A son for a son. No, no. Protect the—"

But that was all, for in the next instant, Tom fired his gun. The bullet hit Armstrong, who had twisted away at the last moment, in the shoulder, and he staggered backward, grabbing out for a piling to steady himself. Brady yelled as Tom fired again and Armstrong disappeared over the side of the wharf, the sound of him splashing into the river reverberating along the wharf, riding on the tail of gunfire.

"What the hell?" Brady yelled, oblivious to anything but a searing sense of unreality. Tom had just plugged Armstrong and was running to the wharf's edge, gun still drawn.

"Put that damn thing away!" Brady yelled as he ran to join Tom.

"I had to do it," Tom said. "You saw."

"Saw what?" Brady snapped as he scanned the rippled surface of the gray water. "Saw you shoot an unarmed man? Radio for help. Hurry, he might just be wounded." He looked around the wharf for something to use to throw to Armstrong should he surface. There wasn't a thing.

"I don't believe you," Tom shouted, gun waving. "Armstrong tried to kill your wife and your son. You know how it works, he would have pled insanity. Sooner or later, he would have come after your family again. I did it for you."

Brady repeated, "Put the gun away." He thought he saw Armstrong surface, but then what he thought was a head disappeared and he wasn't sure. "What you did was shoot a defenseless man," he told Tom. "Get some help out here or I will."

"I covered for you last year," Tom said, sounding aggrieved. Nevertheless, he tucked his revolver into its holster.

Brady, still searching the river, said, "Jason Briggs woke up today and told everyone Billy had a gun the night you and he argued. And I never asked you to cover for me, you know that."

"Jason woke up? He talked?"

"A little. Wait a second. Over there!" Brady yelled as a head popped up out of the water, this time for sure. Armstrong was obviously hurt, but he was just as obviously alive. "He's wounded, Tom. He's crazy and wounded and he's going to drown if you don't do something now. You can save him. We'll figure the rest out later."

"I can't swim," Tom said as they watched Armstrong battle the current with increasingly futile strokes. "What have I done? Oh my God, what have I done?"

Brady was already yanking off his boots. He dropped his cell phone and gun onto the wharf. He zeroed in on Armstrong's position and dived into the river.

The water was surprisingly cold, but the late-summer current wasn't as strong as he'd feared. He allowed that current to sweep him along until he got close enough to Armstrong to take strong strokes in his direction. The current grew weaker and he made good time. He paused to look around. Armstrong had found a small, partially submerged log, which was helping keep him afloat, but he looked ready to let it go and slip under the surface.

"Think of your wife," Brady hollered, swimming faster.

Armstrong's eyes seemed to refocus. Brady got close enough to see the ripped cloth of his left shoulder and the torn flesh beneath. He grabbed hold of Armstrong, anticipating trouble when he told the man to let go of the water-soaked log, but Armstrong did as asked, depending on Brady now. The nearer shore was too industrial. Brady could see no way out of the water over there, so he headed back the way he'd come. Flashing lights meant the police had arrived. Police meant able hands to help him get Armstrong back on the wharf and hopefully to a waiting ambulance.

He tried not to think of Tom as he swam, but his former partner's words haunted him. Tom had done something terrible out of misplaced loyalty. Brady was saving Armstrong as much for Tom's sake as for Armstrong's.

Help came long before he reached the wharf in the form of two officers with a flotation device. Brady left Armstrong with them and swam to the wharf, climbing the rusted metal ladder placed there decades ago as a safety measure for dockworkers.

He found his boots, keys and cell phone where he'd left them, but there was no sign of his gun. He looked around for Tom, but couldn't see him. Tom's partner, Hastings, stood watching the rescue operation, so he approached him.

"Where's Tom?" he asked as he pulled his boots on over his soaking-wet socks.

"I haven't seen him," Hastings said. "His unit isn't here."

"It's out by Armstrong's truck," Brady said.

"No, it isn't. Are you the one who fired the shots?"

"Wait a second, Tom called you—"

"The call came from some guy who heard gunfire. An ambulance is on the way."

Brady stared at Hastings as he tried to make sense of what he was hearing. Tom had found Armstrong's truck but hadn't reported it? He'd gone off on foot in pursuit without alerting backup?

"Is that Bill Armstrong out there in the river?" Hastings said.

"Yeah." What was going through Tom's head?

"Hey, where are you going? You can't leave!" Hastings called as Brady walked away.

Brady didn't respond.

AFTER LOOKING THROUGH the peephole, Lara opened the door to Tom James. His eyes were very bright in his flushed face. He looked as though he'd just run a marathon. Her heart jerked into overdrive. "Is Brady okay?"

"He's fine, he's fine," Tom said.

She glanced across the street where the police officer sat in her patrol car and waved as Tom stepped inside the house.

Tom said, "Officer Alcott knows I'm here. I've come to take you to Brady."

"Why? What do you mean, take me to him? You said he was okay."

"Calm down. Truth is, he saved me from myself this evening. I collared Armstrong down by the river and there was a tussle, no one hurt badly, you understand, but Brady went into the river after Armstrong. Your husband is quite the hero."

Lara studied Tom's eyes. It crossed her mind that he might not appreciate his nonpolice ex-partner stealing some of his thunder. As for herself, she didn't care who caught Bill Armstrong, just that he was caught. She could take a deep breath now, the first in many days.

"Myra ran down to the store, but Gretchen is in the kitchen. I need to tell her I'm leaving," she said over her shoulder as she walked to the blanket she'd spread on the carpeted floor. Nathan lay atop the blanket, kicking bare legs and smiling up at her. She kneeled down to pick him up.

"I'll tell her," Tom said as he disappeared into the kitchen. Lara heard his voice and Gretchen's. She stood with Nathan in her arms, scooping up the diaper bag and the new car seat.

"All set?" Tom asked as he walked back through the kitchen door. Gretchen called out a goodbye.

"All set. But you still haven't told me where we're going to meet Brady."

"Procedure sends everyone who goes into the river over to the hospital, so we'll catch up with him there," Tom said as he took the car seat from Lara. He tickled Nathan's chin and winked at the baby before turning back to Lara. "Don't look so worried, it's just routine. Your husband is fine."

"Thank heavens this is over."

"Exactly," he said, opening the door. "By the way, Brady told me Jason Briggs woke up today."

"Yes. The boy confirmed Billy had a gun with him the night you and Brady chased him. Isn't that a relief?"

"You bet," Tom said, taking her arm. "We're kind of in a hurry," he added as he escorted her across the lawn to his unit.

Lara waved at Officer Alcott as she left, anticipating the moment she saw Brady and they knew this was all behind them. And afterward?

Fear and panic had pushed them together. There had been moments when she knew where her destiny lay, moments without confusion, when everything seemed clear. The only question was—could it last?

BRADY SWITCHED OFF his headlights as he turned onto Tom's long, straight driveway. Through the trees, he saw lights on in the house but no sign of Tom's SUV parked out front. Still, unsure what his friend's state of mind might be at the moment, he decided on a quiet approach and rolled to a stop after turning the engine off.

So, what was he doing here? Had he come to arrest his ex-partner for shooting an unarmed man? He couldn't arrest anyone, Tom had stolen his gun for some crazy reason and besides, he wasn't a cop.

Lara was right. He was a cop, with or without a badge, that's how he thought. That's who and what he was. And right now, he was more a cop than Tom. He retrieved the flashlight from the glove box and got out of the truck.

On his way to the door, he decided to hell with the quiet approach. If Tom was inside he could just answer his door and a whole boatload of questions, too. He'd taken justice into his own hands tonight and sooner or later he'd have to face the music. What was he thinking shooting Armstrong? They needed answers from the man. They needed to know why he shot Jason Briggs and if he burned down Mrs. Beaton's house with her in it and maybe most importantly, what he was guilty of when it came to Karen Wylie.

Repeated banging on the door accomplished nothing. Brady stalked across the yard. He used the flashlight to peer through the window into the dark workshop. There were two cars in evidence, but neither of them was Tom's SUV. The tarp was missing off the small car Brady assumed belonged to Tom's ex-wife. The other car was a dark sedan, about as nondescript as a car could get. Brady had first seen it a few days before with the engine hood up.

He stepped away from the shop then paused. He

turned back and shined the light through the window again. The smaller car looked like the one Nicole Stevens had been driving earlier that day.

It couldn't be. It was the same size as the car he'd seen under the tarp, the one Tom had sworn he was working on for his ex, Caroline. Brady tried every available angle and couldn't see the rear window. The metallic Riverport High School honor-student sticker was all he could think of to connect this car with Nicole.

Why did he want to connect it to Nicole?

Another memory surfaced. He finally remembered where he'd seen Nicole before. Standing on the sidewalk in front of a blue car, talking to Tom. Hair was different, though. Lighter, fluffier. When? Think. In the evening. Not long ago. The night someone shot Jason Briggs.

His brain felt as if it had been caught in a fog for days, if not months. He'd been so focused on his own problems, on Lara and Nathan and then Bill Armstrong's threats that he hadn't thought clearly about other things. What else had he missed?

Okay, so maybe Tom was working on the girl's car for her in his spare time. Or maybe he'd lied about it being his wife's car because he was embarrassed to admit he was screwing around with a seventeen-year-old kid.

"Tom, you pathetic loser," Brady said. He shone the light on the other car now. His light froze on the trunk, which was slightly ajar. The sleeve of a dark blue garment with gold decorations trailed from inside.

Nicole had worn such a garment earlier that day.

Good Lord, was Tom involved with Nicole? Were there two separate issues here: Armstrong's revenge and Tom's lechery?

He had to look at that garment and he had to see the back of the blue car. There was only one window in the shop and a brand-new lock on the door, which meant he would have to break the window to get inside. There would be no way to cover up a broken window.

Wait, there was an additional room attached to the back of the shop. Tom's climate-controlled gun room. Brady couldn't remember if it sported its own door, but if it did, maybe the lock would be older and easier to break. There were also the two big doors through which Tom drove cars into the shop.

Brady set off, keeping close to the perimeter. He passed a row of three steel barrels and an old engine block before coming across the double shop doors. Shining his light over them, he could see they were locked from the inside. He skirted new construction to get to the extension that housed the gun room. No doors, no windows, no nothing.

So, did he walk away?

Hell, no.

But first things first. He knew by now the police would be looking for him. Tom might have gone to turn himself in. Someone would undoubtedly get in touch with Lara, who would then worry. He took out his phone and punched in her number. Her phone rang once then switched to her answering machine and he left a brief message. He called information and got Myra's sister's number then placed that call. Myra answered.

"Lara left with the police," she said. "I wasn't here but Gretchen was. She said one of the officers told her they were going to meet you at the hospital."

Brady frowned. "Which officer?"

He heard Myra ask Gretchen the question. She came back on the line a second later and said, "She doesn't know. A man was all she said."

Brady said, "Did she take Nathan with her?"

"Of course. I don't think you'll be prying the little dear away from her anytime soon."

"You're right," Brady said. "Okay, I'll meet her at the hospital in a little while. I have something to do first."

Using the long-handled flashlight, Brady smashed the shop window. He used the flashlight again to clear the jagged pieces of glass away, then pulled a wheelbarrow close to the window and used it to climb through to the top of the workbench on the other side. Mindful that Tom could show up at any moment, he resisted turning on the bright work lights and made his way to the blue car.

The metallic sticker was right where it had been at three o'clock that afternoon. So, where was Nicole Stevens?

That led him to the trunk of the sedan where he flipped up the trunk and extracted the garment.

A wave of relief flooded him as he realized it wasn't Nicole's blue blouse but Tom's old letterman jacket from college. It, too, was dark blue though a heavier material. The gold decorations were merit badges for three different sports. Just an old jacket. What had he been thinking, casting Tom as some sort of villain?

The jacket felt stiff and was stained dark in places, as though it had been used to absorb a fair amount of some liquid. Brady flashed the light into the trunk, where he found the carpeted floor also stained. A corner had been pried loose as though Tom was preparing to replace the carpet. The light glittered off something small and silver in the middle of the stain.

Setting the jacket aside, Brady picked up the little ornament he now recognized as a pendant shaped like a heart, filled with a light pink shell-like stone.

Once again he had the feeling he should remember something, this time about the little heart. And once again he was stymied. He could see it lying on skin. Not Nicole, she hadn't been wearing a heart bracelet or necklace—and it hit him then with a jolt. Not Nicole. *Karen.*

Karen Wylie had been wearing a necklace when they talked with her at the drugstore. A necklace with a small silver heart. He turned the silver pendant in his hand. This heart. And now the heart was in a trunk stained with something dark...

He fought the conclusion his brain raced toward. It couldn't be blood. That would mean Tom—

Mrs. Beaton wore really thick glasses. From a distance, would Tom letterman's jacket look like a uniform? Would the sports patches look like insignias of some kind? Had Tom been the one to meet Karen and lead her off?

He deposited the jacket on the workbench and searched the shop until he remembered seeing a half-empty water bottle in Nicole's car. He fetched the bottle and poured a little on the stain. A tiny river of red pooled on the piece of sheet metal under the jacket.

His stomach lurched.

Not proof, but together with everything else...

Messing around with girls didn't mean murder. So what was Karen Wylie's necklace doing in the questionably bloody trunk of a car Brady had never seen before? What was Nicole's car doing in Tom's shop?

Okay, so Tom was involved with teenagers. Maybe he did go meet Karen. Maybe as they were driving into Portland, they ran over a dog. Maybe Tom used his jacket to pick up the injured, bleeding animal. Maybe Karen helped. They might have put it in the trunk. Karen's necklace could have caught and broke when they took the dog out at the vet's.

Maybe it wasn't even Tom's car. Brady searched until he found Tom's insurance card on the visor. Okay, it was Tom's car, but the scenario, while not plausible, was surely possible enough to cut his ex-partner a little slack. Wasn't it?

His phone rang. Lara's number glowed on the screen, but the voice that answered his greeting wasn't hers.

It was Tom's.

Chapter Thirteen

"I know you're at my house," Tom said.

Brady flinched, wondering if Tom used a hidden surveillance camera. And then the choice of Tom's words struck him. He'd said house, not shop. He must have seen Brady's truck parked outside the house. He said, "Why are you using Lara's phone? Where is she?"

"She's here with me. So is Nathan."

"Where exactly is 'here,' Tom? What's going on?"

"So, hero, did you save Bill Armstrong?"

"Yeah, I did. Listen, I haven't talked to the police yet. If you go to Dixon and explain how you got a little too anxious—"

Tom laughed. "You don't lie very well, partner."

Brady took a deep breath. All he had was a bunch of unanswered questions. He said, "How about you and I sit down and talk this through? Lara and Nathan don't need to be involved. We can figure something out."

"You're right. There are things we need to talk about. I underestimated your tenacity and your sheer stubbornness. You come to me, I'll just keep Lara and Nathan here as insurance."

"What the hell does that mean?" Brady snapped.

"Why did you leave the wharf, why did you take my gun?"

"Isn't it obvious?" Tom said.

Brady took a steadying breath. "Explain it to me."

"Not now, later. I want you to fill your truck with gas and drive out to that house you're building. You and I can talk. I'm not going to the police and I strongly suggest, for your family's sake, you don't either. Is that clear enough? Oh, and I wouldn't dawdle if I were you."

"Tom, man, don't throw away your life because of one mistake, don't—"

The phone went dead.

Brady swore as he punched off the phone. He rifled Tom's workbench looking for tools. He wasn't going to confront Tom unarmed, not after what he'd seen him do that day and the troubling evidence in the shop, and now he'd taken Lara and Nathan! He needed a gun. And if Tom hadn't changed things around, there was an arsenal behind the padlocked door in the back of the shop.

He found a chisel and a mallet. They would have to do. He sidled around the two cars and moved toward the back where he made short work of the padlock.

He swung the door inward and turned on the light as there was no reason to fear Tom coming back now.

And stopped dead in his tracks.

Tom had turned his gun room into a trophy room.

LARA TRIED to think of one smart decision she'd made in the last several days and couldn't come up with a thing.

Clutching a mercifully sleeping Nathan to her chest, she closed her eyes. She was sitting on the floor in the corner of a dark walk-in closet. It was stuffy, pitch-black and hot. Her lip throbbed. Even her arm hurt after a day of not bothering her at all.

Tom had her phone. He'd told her he was going to call Brady to come get her. She knew he was setting a trap for Brady, she just wasn't sure why.

After Tom picked her up, they'd driven out of town, away from people and buildings. He made up excuses for not going to the hospital. As Nathan grew increasingly fussy, she grew suspicious. How could she get herself and her frantic baby, strapped into his car seat and then into the backseat, out of the police car? All the locks were controlled by the driver. She'd tried to stay calm as she begged Tom to stop so she could comfort Nathan, but Tom had ignored her.

At last she realized they were going to his house. She'd been there once, with Brady, and even then she'd found it a remote and lonely place. The thought of visiting it at night with Tom acting the way he was made her queasy. How could she stop him?

He'd driven toward the house from a different approach. When his headlights swept over the yard before the driveway intersected the road, she'd caught sight of Brady's old truck and hope had soared in her heart like a Fourth of July rocket. It had died just as quickly.

Tom hadn't even slowed down, but he'd finally started talking, and the venom that came out of his mouth had stunned Lara down to her core. And terrified her. Tom blamed Brady for things Lara didn't even understand. He kept saying Brady wouldn't quit, Brady would keep pushing and pushing, Brady had ruined everything.

Brady would pay.

When Lara had tried to reason with him he'd spared

a hand from the wheel to backhand her across the face. He'd split her lip open, but he'd also shut her up.

And then they finally stopped and he herded her into the closet at gunpoint, taking her purse and her cell phone in the bargain. Nathan had finally fallen asleep at her breast and now lay against her, his forehead moist against her neck, his breathing noisy from a nose stuffed up from all the crying. She didn't know what was coming next, only that Tom was off his rocker.

And she and Nathan were in mortal danger.

The door opened suddenly, blinding her with light.

"Tom," she said, throwing an arm up to ward off the glare. Please—"

"Get up," he interrupted. "We're going to get ready for Brady. I told you I'd call him to come get you." As she stood up, he grabbed Nathan from her arms. The baby awoke with a startled cry. Lara tried to take him back. Tom pushed her away with the heel of his hand. She stumbled backward into a wall, hitting her head, causing stars to appear. He strode off with Nathan.

There was no handy shovel or two-by-four with which to hit him over the back of the head. There was nothing to do but stagger after him.

For now.

THE GUN ROOM HAD UNDERGONE a terrible transformation since the last time Brady had visited.

The guns were still there, kept now behind a locked glass door in a cabinet designed to display them for best effect. A computer had been added, the accompanying desk pushed up against the west wall and littered with electronic equipment including two printers and several cameras.

What stole the show, however, were the dozens of photographs pinned to the walls, all depicting naked or nearly naked young women, some posed playfully, some engaged in sex acts, some in chains, some bound, eyes wide with real or feigned terror.

Jason Briggs had said he'd seen naked pictures of Karen Wylie. Brady took in a half-dozen different faces, including Karen's and Nicole's.

A picture above the desk was one of the more disturbing images. A female was bolted to the wall in shackles and chains. Her eyes were closed, bright red blood trailed from a slash across bare breasts.

Sara Armstrong.

There was a man in this photo as there were in a few of the others. He held a whip and wore a mask, but Brady knew it was Tom. Same build, same coloring, same tattoo on his left buttock. Brady strode across the room in three steps, tore the picture from the wall, wadded it up and threw it across the room. Taking a deep breath, he forced himself to leave everything else as it was.

He used the flashlight to break the glass in the gun cabinet. Tom fancied himself a connoisseur of handguns and there were several to choose from. Brady retrieved a Glock very much like his own. A .38 came next, a gun Brady often tucked into his boot. At the last minute, he also pulled a derringer from the case. Just like in the Old West, the derringer was small enough to palm. Even the .22 Magnum bullets were small, and though the shot would have to be damn near point-blank to cause deadly harm, in a pinch, it might come in handy. He grabbed Tom's dog tags off a hook inside the case. He found ammunition for all three weapons from a drawer below the case.

Inside an adjoining rifle case, he saw an AK–47. Would ballistic tests show that was the gun used to shoot Jason Briggs? Brady no longer had any doubts they would.

Among other things, he now suspected his former partner was a cold-blooded killer.

Brady turned toward the bare overhead lightbulb to load the guns, and that's when he saw a narrow door set in the corner. It was locked from the outside and needed a key. He recalled the new construction he'd seen when he walked around the building.

No time to satisfy idle curiosity…

And yet there was something about a door leading off a room like this that raised the hair on the back of Brady's neck. He took the time to hide the derringer and the .38, then used the revolver to shoot the padlock, making sure it was backed by the door frame first. The blast boomeranged around the enclosed room. Brady kicked in the door, ears still ringing.

A rumpled bed dominated the small space, covered with blue satin, stained and rumpled, backed by a pale yellow wall. Mirrors were positioned overhead and lights hung from the ceiling. A movie camera on a tripod pointed at the bed. The doors of the cupboards against the far wall stood ajar. Brady caught a glimpse of chains, whips, handcuffs, eyebolts.

As he stood there taking in the fact his ex-partner was running some kind of underage porno ring, he heard a noise coming from the far side of the bed. He crossed the room in a second.

A woman lay on the floor, stark naked, gagged and bound hand and foot, eyes wide with terror, features smeared with blood. It took a second for the brightly colored tips of her hair to register on Brady's brain. Nicole Stevens.

He stuck the Glock in the holster he still wore on his hip, grabbed the satin cover off the bed and draped it over her. Then he helped her onto the mattress. She began crying as he gently tugged the gag from her mouth.

"He'll come back, he said he would, we have to get out of here," she whispered, her words clipped like staccato notes. "Please, please, get me out of here, help me."

"He's not coming back," Brady said, taking out his pocketknife and hacking the tape binding her wrists. "Are you hurt?"

"Not too bad," she said through her tears. "I just want to go home, please."

Brady sawed at the tape around her ankles. If he called for emergency help, Tom might hear on the squad car radio and know the extent of what Brady had seen. He'd probably figure it out anyway when and if he saw all the guns, but there was no reason to alert him prematurely.

Brady couldn't leave Nicole, though, and he couldn't let her drive her car away even if he did know how to get the doors open, even if she was in any shape to drive. Like the pictures in the other room, the cars constituted evidence.

"Does Tom know where you live?" he asked as Nicole wrapped the spread tighter around herself and stood on wobbly legs.

"Yes. Where are my clothes?"

"I don't know. There isn't time to worry about them. Think of somewhere else I can take you. Somewhere between here and the south side of town." It seemed like hours had passed since the phone call, but when he checked his watch, he found only nine minutes had ticked by. Since he had no intention of putting gas in the truck, he was okay.

Nicole came up with the name of a friend who lived on the way to the Good Neighbors house. She started talking, her voice jittery at first, as soon as they were in the truck and moving away from Tom's place.

"He caught me in a DUI," she said, her gaze darting between Brady and the road ahead. "It wasn't the first time. He offered me a deal. All I had to do was have sex with him on camera. He said he filmed it for himself, you know, to look at later, but I heard him talking one day and I know he really sold it on the Internet. At first I said no, but then he told me how I would have a police record and how I wouldn't be able to get into college or anything and I thought of my parents, especially my dad, and well, eventually, I agreed."

Brady's hands tightened on the wheel. All those times he'd thought Tom was giving kids warnings instead of tickets, he'd actually been recruiting.

"When I got to his place, I saw pictures of Karen and Sara on the wall. I remembered a couple of months before Sara killed herself that she told me she'd been busted smoking dope at a party. She said she'd made a deal and it was going to be okay. And Karen thought she was going to be a damn movie star."

Brady took a corner fast. Nicole clutched the satin spread in one hand, the door handle in the other.

"After I talked to Ms. Kirk today, I decided I wasn't going to make any more movies," Nicole said, once again dissolving into tears. She finally added, "So I went over there to tell him I was quitting and that if he said a word about the DUI, I was going to tell the cops on him because Karen is gone and where is she? I think he knows."

"And that's when he started beating you," Brady said.

"He…he raped me, too," she mumbled. "And he filmed it all. The beating, the rape, me screaming. He liked it. He said he'd come back later and finish the job. When I heard you poking around and breaking things, I thought it was him. When that gun went off I almost died."

So, she'd put two and two together, which was more than Brady could take credit for. He'd been so wound up in his own troubles he hadn't seen what was going on with his old partner in his own backyard.

I hear voices, Armstrong had said over and over again. *Voices, telling me what to do.* And as soon as he'd seen Brady he'd mumbled something about trying to protect Nathan. In the next instant, Tom shot him. At that moment, Tom hadn't known about Jason Briggs waking up. If he was responsible for shooting Jason as well as corrupting Bill Armstrong, he might have thought he could still save himself.

Had Tom fired the shot out of anger as he claimed, or had he fired it to save his skin? Was it possible Tom had been feeding Bill Armstrong directions to hasten his mental disintegration? Had Armstrong started the fires thinking in some convoluted way he was exacting justice? Was it possible Armstrong had tried to take Nathan to protect him from Tom, not to harm him?

Hell, anything was possible. The world was upside down. Tom had forsaken his oath to serve and protect and become a child molester and Internet purveyor, Karen Wylie might well be dead, he'd beaten Nicole to a pulp, he'd shot a man in cold blood and now he'd kidnapped Lara and Nathan.

Brady pulled up in front of Nicole's friend's house with screeching brakes. "Go inside. Call the cops and tell them everything you know."

"I can't," she said, shivering despite the eighty-degree night.

"You have to. There's no hiding this. You have to face it."

"But I think he hurt Karen—"

"So do I. Call the police. Get them to go out to Tom's place. I'll take care of Tom."

For a second he paused. Should he have the girl tell them about the Good Neighbors house? And risk a horde of police showing up with sirens blaring?

No way.

He left in a hurry, senses heightened, ready for battle. There wasn't a doubt in his mind blood would be spilled that night. It was up to him to make sure not a drop of it was innocent.

LARA WAS in the dark again, only this time she was outside. A light suspended from a tree branch hung directly over her head, but remained unlit.

Tom had strapped Nathan back into his car seat and left him inside the house where his cries couldn't be heard. Then he'd gagged her and all but carried her toward the river where he'd thrown her into a heavy wooden chair. He'd bound her with tape and left her there.

It was a nightmare.

Tom was gunning for Brady, and Brady was on his way. She was bait, sitting out by the river, trussed up like a sacrificial goat, set to lure the man she loved to his death.

It was up to Brady. She closed her eyes for a second, then opened them wide. She'd just heard a sound.

Brady?

No. The shape illuminated by the sliver of moon revealed a man the same size as Brady, but it wasn't him. The gait was wrong, this man was heavier. Tom. He held something bulky, like Nathan's car seat. Straining for a sound from her baby, she heard nothing but footfalls traversing the rubble-strewn landscape.

And the thundering beat of her own heart.

BRADY STOPPED the truck long before turning onto River Road. It was a rural area, no nearby houses, not yet. They would come later. He pulled on the light jacket he kept behind the seat and got out of the truck.

It would take the police a few minutes to respond to Nicole's call. Dixon would be notified. He'd probably hurry out to Tom's place. The whole force would eventually end up out there. Miles from here. A good thirty minutes.

He took off at a trot, reaching the dark house within moments. If the squad car was at the house, it had been pulled inside the garage.

If all Tom wanted was a means of escape, then he'd have left in the squad car. He'd had lots of lead time. He didn't need to take Lara or Nathan, he didn't need Brady's truck. He could have disappeared into Portland within an hour or two.

Brady had had a little time to think as he drove. A couple of hours had passed between the shooting down at the wharf and Tom calling on Lara's phone. By the time he made that call, he'd already decided to involve Lara and Nathan, he'd already collected them.

Brady surmised Tom hadn't been sure what he wanted to do until he'd seen Brady's truck in his driveway and figured the game was up, there was no getting away, the police would be looking for him, he'd waited too long to make a clean escape. If all he wanted was hostages, he would have just taken Lara and Nathan. So what he wanted in addition to hostages was revenge.

The why was what Brady didn't know.

He snuck up under the front window and peeked inside the house. No lights, no movement. He had already taken the Glock out of the holster and held the weapon in his right hand. He moved silently to the door and found it unlatched. He pushed it open.

The house had an empty, silent-as-a-tomb feel to it. He moved through the rooms carefully. He found a baby blanket near the walk-in closet under the stairs and he stared at it for a count of ten, his heart in his throat. Then he continued a systematic search of the dark house until he got to the bedroom in the back. As he glanced out the window toward the river, a light came on.

Lara sat in a wooden chair under a work light hooked up to an electrical cord strung between the house and the river. She was bound and gagged, like Nicole, though mercifully, unlike Nicole, she hadn't been stripped and beaten. Her eyes looked terrified. Tears he'd actually wanted to see at one time now streamed down her face. There was no sign of Tom or Nathan.

He knelt down on the floor, took out his phone and punched in Chief Dixon's number. It was time to give Lara and Nathan an insurance policy in case he failed.

"Dixon here," was the prompt reply.

"Chief, this is Brady Skye. Listen carefully. I'm at a new construction at 555 River Circle. Tom James has my wife and son. I'm going in to get them." He hung up the phone before the questions could start and turned it off, leaving it on the bedroom floor.

It would take a half hour for Dixon to respond. If he was lucky. If Dixon didn't write the call off as a prank.

He wound his way back through the empty house to the sliding glass door at the back. The undeveloped yard appeared empty, though it was heavily shadowed.

So, Lara was the bait.

A movement behind her caught his attention. Tom, moving into the light, holding a baby seat in one hand, a gun pointed at the back of Lara's head with the other. The faint cries of an infant assaulted Brady's ears.

He hadn't outwitted Tom. Tom had anticipated what Brady would do, and now held all the cards.

"Come on out," Tom shouted. "We've been waiting for you."

For the first time in his life, Brady hoped Chief Dixon would show his face. He opened the door and stepped outside.

LARA DID HER BEST to stop crying as she watched Brady approach, so strong and capable looking in boots, jeans and a light jacket. She could communicate with nothing but her eyes and she tried, with her expression, to apologize for being so naive and stupid and endangering them all. And to tell him she loved him and trusted him and yet didn't expect him to be able to pull this particular hat out of this particular fire. The issues she'd had with the way Brady handled life now seemed insignificant. Great eleventh-hour insights.

Brady met her gaze once and then didn't look at her again. Thankfully, Nathan had grown quiet, though his stuffy breathing reached her ears every few seconds. She could tell by Brady's expression he was plotting and planning his next move.

"What the hell do you think you're doing?" Brady asked, coming to a stop a few feet away.

"Getting even," Tom said as he came around from her left. Her gaze immediately went to the baby whose eyes were closed, his cheeks flushed and damp. He'd apparently cried himself to sleep. Tom pointed the gun at the baby's head.

Lara gasped, though the sound was swallowed in the gag.

Brady took a step forward.

"Stop right there, partner. You know about Karen Wylie, don't you?"

Lara hadn't expected to hear Karen's name. Her gaze flew to Brady.

Brady said, "I'm guessing you killed her."

"It had to be done."

"I know about Nicole, too. So do the police."

"Then we'll make this short and sweet," Tom said. "Walk right over there and put all the hardware on the ground. That includes the .38 in your boot. My .38, right?"

"You know me too well," Brady said.

Tom laughed. "You're a predictable SOB. Now, do it slow and so I can see you. I have an itchy finger and this baby's skull looks kind of fragile."

Brady disarmed himself slowly, laying the Glock down first, then carefully extracting the .38 from his boot. Watching him, Lara died a little inside, not only for her chances and Nathan's but for Brady. He'd told her once he would never disarm himself for a gunman, that he'd prefer to take his chances. He was doing this for them. He was giving his life for them.

How it must irk him to surrender control. She felt new tears burn her nose and sting her eyes.

"Now, come free your wife's hands. And don't try to be a hero."

Brady walked up to Lara and started unwinding the tape. He looked at her once and smiled, then he looked at Tom. "Just tell me why," he said.

"You haven't figured it out?"

"Not all of it. I think I know what you've done, I just don't know why you're gunning for me."

"I hate to admit it, but I've been playing catch-up ever since you shot Billy Armstrong."

Brady took off the last of the tape, his fingers lingering on Lara's wrist for a moment, the touch tender, like a goodbye.

Tom yanked him by the back of the shirt. "That's enough." He threw a pair of handcuffs at Lara. "Turn around, let the little lady handcuff you. And do it right, honey, or your baby gets it."

Lara picked up the cuffs with numb fingers. Brady turned around, his hands behind his back. She looped the handcuffs on his wrists, trying to see if there was a way to make them loose enough for him to escape. But Tom yanked Brady around again and the cuffs clicked into place.

"Very nice," Tom said. With the gun now pointed at Brady, he handed Nathan to Lara, whose feet were still tied to one another and to the chair. She took the baby with a flood of relief and held him close as if she could protect him with her love.

Brady turned around and faced her, his eyes dark and consuming. Tom, the gun still in one hand, patted Brady down head to toe. Apparently convinced Brady was now harmless, he said, "Figured it out yet?"

"Most of it. I saw you talking to Nicole Stevens a

half hour before Jason Briggs was shot. How did you change cars so fast?"

"I didn't. I used to carry the AK-47 in the squad car trunk."

"You shot him from your squad car? That was taking a terrible chance."

"Maybe," Tom said smugly.

"I'm guessing you burned up that poor old woman in Scottsdell, too."

"Snoopy bitch. Who knows what she might have remembered the next day."

"Like seeing the sedan you drove the day you promised Karen Wylie you'd meet her bus in Scottsdell and whisk her away to Hollywood? It's her blood in the trunk, isn't it? Where'd you dump her body?"

"She's in one of the barrels behind my shop. One more time, partner. Have you figured out why?"

"Why you corrupted Bill Armstrong into starting the fires and lurking around and making threats? Why you kept me running all over the place, too worried to think straight?"

"And don't forget your dear old father. I hired a couple of punks to pick a fight. The old man has gotten soft."

Brady said, "All to protect your little movie empire, am I right?"

Tom laughed again. "Partly. It actually started with what Billy yelled at me down by the river the night you so kindly shot the brat."

"What he yelled? It was gobbledygook. He was upset about his sister's suicide. He was drunk."

"Not really. You know, you've been a major pain in the neck for a year now," Tom said.

"You were talking about Billy," Brady said softly. "What he told you—"

"He saw his sister's pictures on the Internet. He confronted her about it. The little tramp told Billy I was behind it."

"You were behind it," Brady repeated.

Tom shrugged. Lara saw Brady's gaze travel to the weapon in Tom's hand. His eyes grew steely. "Where'd you get that gun, partner?" he said.

Tom laughed. "Finally, you see the light."

"You took it off Billy's body. You knelt by him and you stole the gun because you were afraid I overheard him accuse you of driving his sister to kill herself."

"More than that. He figured out I forced her to take her grandma's pills. I had no choice. The girl started making noise about telling her father everything."

Lara twisted to see the weapon. She had to assume it was Billy's grandfather's .45-caliber Colt automatic. The gun the boys had found and lusted over. The gun Billy had taken with him the night he and Jason stole the beer and the car, the gun he'd had on him when providence delivered both him and Tom James to a lonely riverbank.

Brady said, "I shot the wrong person, didn't I? I should have let the kid plug you. You'd already murdered his sister, but at least Karen Wylie would still be alive. And Mrs. Beaton."

"Hindsight," Tom said, "is cheap."

"You set me up. You wanted to keep me so off balance I wouldn't stop to think about what I heard, so you stole the gun from his dead body."

"I was going to dump it later, but it's a beauty."

"And that's why you shot Jason, because you knew he knew about the gun and you figured he was going to tell Lara about it. What he was really trying to do was to get Lara to talk to Karen about posing nude. He'd seen her pictures, I guess while in juvie. And maybe Billy had told him about what you got his sister to do."

"They need to keep a better eye on the inmates' computer habits."

"And then you started feeding Bill Armstrong a bunch of lies and fueling his grief to escalate his threats, to keep me from thinking straight. And when he tried to tell me what was happening, you tried to kill him. And failed."

Tom shrugged again.

"I never heard what Billy said to you that night," Brady said. "I just heard Sara's name. Nothing else."

"I thought for sure you'd heard some of it. Well, no matter, it's all worked out okay."

Brady shook his head. "You call what you've done working out okay? The misery you've caused, the death and the destruction? And now you're stuck here in Riverport because you were too stupid or too vain to leave when you could, and all that is what you call working out okay?"

Tom's voice turned razor sharp. "I'm taking your wife and your kid and using them to get out of here and you're going to the bottom of the river with a bullet in your gut. So, yeah, after the pain in the neck you've been, it's all good."

Lara closed her eyes as Tom raised the gun.

She heard Brady say, "We've gone through a lot together, you and me, Tom. How about letting me say goodbye to my wife and son?"

Lara's eyes popped open. Tom seemed to consider the ramifications of Brady's request and finally said, "Sure, why not? Just make it quick."

Brady approached her, hands secured behind his back. Leaning down he brushed his lips against her cheek.

She managed with one hand to pull the gag from her mouth. "I love you," she said.

He leaned a little closer and looked tenderly at Nathan. Then he glanced back at her. "Dog tags," he said so softly she thought for sure she'd misunderstood. She met his gaze. His eyes bored into her. Dog tags? He wasn't wearing any she could see, but of course, he wore a zipped-up jacket—

In August?

As he kissed Nathan's forehead, she did the only thing she could think of. She moved her hand up under his jacket and shirt, and felt the skin-warmed steel of a small gun dangling from his neck. Her fingers curled around the grip and she yanked as he straightened up. The gun and chain slipped into her hand and she covered it with Nathan's blanket. She switched off the safety as he'd taught her to do years before.

"I love you," he said, giving her the time to slip her hand around the grip, his voice covering the sound of her pulling back the hammer. "No matter what, I love you." Turning, he stepped aside.

It was up to her. He'd given her the means, now she had to make it happen. With a steely determination she never knew she possessed, she pointed the tiny gun at Tom.

And fired.

"I WAS HOPING he would be in too big a hurry to pat down my chest," Brady said. "We got lucky. And you saved us."

Lara snuggled against his side. If she closed her eyes, she could still see Tom James laying at her feet, blood gushing out of the bullet hole in his chest. She kept her eyes wide open.

"He's going to make it," Brady said as though reading her mind. "Chief Dixon said he survived the surgery. He'll get a trial and hopefully, he'll rot in jail."

Her lips curved into a smile against the downy softness of her son's head. They were seated in Brady's living room, decompressing after hours of standing around in the dark. The TV played softly in the background, turned on to provide background noise as she worked to get Nathan to sleep, left on out of pure inertia.

Lara had spoken to her mother, who had aborted her trip upon learning of the fire that destroyed her house. She'd flown home and was now ensconced at the downtown hotel. Brady again seemed to read her mind as he said, "Let's have a wedding."

"We're already married," she said, looking up at him.

He hugged her tighter. "I feel as though we cheated your mother out of a wedding. If she still wants one, let's go through with it, the bigger and messier the better."

Lara laughed softly. "It might help her forget we burned down her house."

"For a while, anyway. Hey. Maybe she'll hire me to rebuild it for her."

Lara smiled again. She'd heard Chief Dixon offer Brady his old job back. She was betting money Brady would give up contracting and return to his true vocation before long, though she really didn't care what he did as long as it made him happy. She said, "You still haven't reached your father?" When he shook his head, she added, "The bars closed hours ago."

"I know."

"And Garrett?"

"He doesn't answer his phone, either."

She settled into the cushions. She knew daylight would bring at least one decision. Would they stay in Riverport or move to Seattle? The one thing they didn't have to decide was whether or not they were a family.

For Lara, that question had been answered hours before when she sat in a dark closet, anticipating Brady's arrival, knowing he was walking into a trap and she was powerless to save him. And knowing that if he died, so would she. He was her man just as she was his woman. There was no one else for either of them. There never would be.

It had been cinched when he gave up control of the situation and handed it to her. Thank heavens she'd come through.

She said, "Next time, *you* shoot the bad guy, okay?"

He kissed her tenderly. "Okay."

"Because I don't care for it."

"I know." He leaned his head against hers. They should go to bed, but neither of them had the energy to move. Her mind drifted until Brady's body suddenly stiffened, "Where's the remote?" he asked, a note of urgency in his voice. "I just saw Garrett's face on the news. Something about a bomb."

She dug for the remote and turned up the volume. The picture on the screen showed the face of an attractive woman with intelligent deep-set gray eyes. The announcer said "—over the sudden death of forty-one-year-old Reno attorney Elaine Greason."

"What's this got to do with Garrett?"

"I don't know."

"Greason was killed in a car bomb yesterday morning." A new picture filled the box above the newscaster's left shoulder. Lara drew in her breath as Brady jumped to his feet.

Garrett's picture seemed to fill the screen. The newscaster said, "Once again, police are looking for this man, Garrett Skye, Greason's bodyguard. Police caution Skye should be considered armed and dangerous."

As the news moved on to the next big story, Lara got to her feet, juggling Nathan and his blankets. Brady stared at the floor, a knot in his jaw.

She said, "Garrett wouldn't kill anyone—"

Brady turned to her. "Wouldn't he? What if someone paid him? He was desperate to get his little girl back. What if he saw this as his only way?"

"I can't believe that."

"But they said—"

She put her free arm around him. "Things aren't always as they seem. You'll help him, won't you?"

"Of course I will." He wrapped her in his arms.

They stood in silence for a long time, Lara's cheek pressed against his chest, his heartbeat drumming in her ear.

There would be bumps, there would be problems— what life came trouble free? But they would face everything, the good, the bad, all of it, together.

* * * * *

Next month be sure to pick up Garrett Skye's story,
BODYGUARD FATHER,
part of Alice Sharpe's two-book series
SKYE BROTHER BABIES.
Look for it only in Harlequin Intrigue!

HARLEQUIN®

American ★ Romance®

CATHY McDAVID
Cowboy Dad

THE STATE OF PARENTHOOD

Natalie Forrester's job at Bear Creek Ranch
is to make everyone welcome, which is an
easy task when it comes to Aaron Reyes—the
unwelcome cowboy and part-owner. His
tenderness toward Natalie's infant daughter
melts the single mother's heart. What's not
so easy to accept is that falling for him means
giving up her job, her family and the only
home she's ever known....

Available August
wherever books are sold.

LOVE, HOME & HAPPINESS

REQUEST YOUR FREE BOOKS!

2 FREE NOVELS PLUS 2 FREE GIFTS!

◆ HARLEQUIN®

INTRIGUE®

Breathtaking Romantic Suspense

YES! Please send me 2 FREE Harlequin Intrigue® novels and my 2 FREE gifts (gifts are worth about $10). After receiving them, if I don't wish to receive any more books, I can return the shipping statement marked "cancel." If I don't cancel, I will receive 6 brand-new novels every month and be billed just $4.24 per book in the U.S. or $4.99 per book in Canada, plus 25¢ shipping and handling per book and applicable taxes, if any*. That's a savings of close to 15% off the cover price! I understand that accepting the 2 free books and gifts places me under no obligation to buy anything. I can always return a shipment and cancel at any time. Even if I never buy another book from Harlequin, the two free books and gifts are mine to keep forever.

182 HDN EEZ7   382 HDN EEZK

Name	(PLEASE PRINT)	
Address		Apt. #
City	State/Prov.	Zip/Postal Code

Signature (if under 18, a parent or guardian must sign)

Mail to the **Harlequin Reader Service:**
IN U.S.A.: P.O. Box 1867, Buffalo, NY 14240-1867
IN CANADA: P.O. Box 609, Fort Erie, Ontario L2A 5X3

Not valid to current subscribers of Harlequin Intrigue books.

Want to try two free books from another line?
Call 1-800-873-8635 or visit www.morefreebooks.com.

* Terms and prices subject to change without notice. N.Y. residents add applicable sales tax. Canadian residents will be charged applicable provincial taxes and GST. Offer not valid in Quebec. This offer is limited to one order per household. All orders subject to approval. Credit or debit balances in a customer's account(s) may be offset by any other outstanding balance owed by or to the customer. Please allow 4 to 6 weeks for delivery. Offer available while quantities last.

Your Privacy: Harlequin is committed to protecting your privacy. Our Privacy Policy is available online at www.eHarlequin.com or upon request from the Reader Service. From time to time we make our lists of customers available to reputable third parties who may have a product or service of interest to you. If you would prefer we not share your name and address, please check here. ☐

HI08R

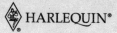
HARLEQUIN®

INTRIGUE®

COMING NEXT MONTH

#1077 THE SHERIFF'S SECRETARY by Carla Cassidy

Sheriff Lucas Jamison and secretary Mariah Harrington had always butted heads. But with her son's life in danger, Mariah trusts the sheriff to uncover a kidnapper hiding in their peaceful community—no matter the secrets revealed.

#1078 DANGEROUSLY ATTRACTIVE by Jenna Ryan

With a killer terrorizing police detective Vanessa Connor, Rick Maguire was assigned to protect her. But the enticing federal agent had to lead her further into danger if she was ever to be safe again.

#1079 A DOCTOR-NURSE ENCOUNTER by Carol Ericson

A relationship between Nurse Lacey Kirk and Dr. Nick Marino had always been expressly forbidden. But nothing could keep them apart amidst a string of deadly cover-ups and patients with secret identities.

#1080 UNDER SUSPICION, WITH CHILD by Elle James

The Curse of Raven's Cliff

Pregnant and alone, Jocelyne Baker believed her love life had been cursed. Yet only fate could have led her into the arms of Andrei Lagios. The cop wore away her defenses, even as the rest of the town grew wary of Jocelyne's return to town.

#1081 BENEATH THE BADGE by Rita Herron

The Silver Star of Texas: Cantara Hills Investigation

Nothing mattered more to Hayes Keller than the badge he wore. But while protecting heiress Taylor Landis, the heart of a real man in need of a good woman was soon exposed.

#1082 BODYGUARD FATHER by Alice Sharpe

Skye Brother Babies

Garrett Skye had a habit of taking on bad assignments, and now he was on the run. But he wasn't willing to leave his baby daughter behind, and that meant taking a stand with teacher Annie Ryder at his side.

HICNM0708